THE GOLDEN BOX

THE GOLDEN BOX

Cassie A. Hunter Macedo

Printed in the United States of America

ISBN 979-8-89114-103-2 (sc)
ISBN 979-8-89114-104-9 (hc)
ISBN 979-8-89114-105-6 (e)

Library of Congress Control Number: 2024912938

2025.03.03

MainSpring Books
5901 W. Century Blvd
Suite 750
Los Angeles, CA, US, 90045

www.mainspringbooks.com

I would like to dedicate my first novel to my nephews Geoffrey and Garred Strole. You both are not only my handsome nephews but also the reason I became a pirate. I sit back and laugh at all the pirate pizza parties we had in the middle of my living room, detailing our treasure maps. It was so easy to babysit you both because I knew we'd have a blast and adventure. It's funny, you guys never wanted to leave, and when you got home, you drove your mom a little crazy, making sounds with your mouth. You took playtime to a whole another level. I see in both of you little bits of me, and it makes me laugh. You are the apple of my eye. Overnight I became an aunt /mom without any pain. Haha. I clearly am the cooler mom. Don't tell your mom (my sister) that I said that. Thank you for always keeping me young and creative. We had a great time growing up together.

I would also like to thank my mom and grandparents (momo and papa pirtle) for being directly responsible for my creative abilities. Many aspects of this story came from their memory and my mom as a child. Thank you to my sister for lifting me when I most needed. Thank you to my special friends who helped me directly. I love you for your unconditional love. Thank you everybody for all the moral support. I couldn't have done it without each and every one of you.

Main characters: Bobby Schutzer, Jason Ferrahi, Jody Jenkins, Sarah Fruentz, and Adam Garcia

Chapter 1

It was fall in 1945 in a small town located in Kalamazoo, Michigan, with a population of 17,094. The town's architecture was very Victorian style—late 1700s. The houses were prominently single level, but some were two-story with wooden shake roofs and bricks that would line the entryway and/or usually the front part of the house. The houses looked like gingerbreads with red fireplaces. Their steep-line roofing came to points like a steeple on an old church. The trees umbrellaed over the street, barely allowing light to shine through. Some houses had fenced front yards, but for the most part, all of the houses had open front yard with manicured short-trimmed landscape. The back yards were enclosed by a six-foot vertical red wooden board type of fencing for privacy. An alleyway separated the back of each house. Two metal garbage cans generally were sitting in the back of the garage and picked up once a week. Some houses had small one-car garages.

Fall was the most beautiful time of the year in Kalamazoo. The leaves on the trees turned beautifully brilliant colors of orange, yellow, and blood red tones. During fall, the trees turn colors and start to fall off the trees and onto the grass and streets. When a car would pass through the neighborhood, the leaves fluttered up like little butterflies. The young kids in the neighborhood would rake the leaves into a big pile and hide or jump into the middle of them. It wasn't uncommon to see the kids playing in the leaves for hours, kicking them and tossing them into the air with laughter.

There was a small bunch of kids that would hang out with each other. There were four of them, but only two of them had bicycles, so if they rode their bikes around, they would let the other one ride on the back or sit on the handlebars. They were twelve to thirteen years old, and all were in the same grade; two boys and two girls. Their names were Bobby Schutzer, who had red-orange hair and blue eyes and freckles, with a stocky body build and an average height for his age, and acted super silly most of the time; Jason Ferrahi, an Italian boy with dark hair and green eyes, thin in build, shorter than Bobby by two inches, and all the girls seemed to have crushes on him; Jody Jenkins, long straight blond hair, beautiful blue eyes, thin, and of average height with perfect white teeth; and Sarah Fruentz, a little Hispanic girl with slightly curly jet-black hair. She spoke English and Spanish, and she had gorgeous brown caramel eyes and eyes shaped like almonds.

They all met every Wednesday. Bobby and Jody would bring their bikes and go to Sarah's house then to Jason's. They would always carry backpacks filled with different items. They'd go to the schoolyard and toss a baseball with each other for a bit then go to the little country convenience store down the street and buy two soda pops and candy bars and bubble gum pieces to share. Then they'd ride back to the baseball field and hang out in the dugout and talk about different stuff. Their conversations usually were lighthearted and always mingled with laughter. They'd talk about their parents, other kids, teachers, school projects, and items they found that were neat. Bobby yelled out, "Did you guys find anything exciting this week?" Jason reached into his jean pockets and pulled out a handful of items: four pennies, a safety pin, a chipped marble, two dice, and what looked like a part of a gear.

Jody yelled out, "I found a doll and a few jacks."

Sarah twirled her hair and said, "Uuh, I found an old key, hee hee." She giggled.

Bobby replied, "Neat! Let's put what we found in a box, and each time, we'll gather items and collect and save them."

Jody yelled out, "Hey, Bobby, what did you find?"

He mumbled, "Oh, nothing really, just a broken Matchbox collectible toy car and half a deck of playing cards, nothing really." So they all put their stuff in a cardboard box and closed it up.

Jason said, "I'll hide the box in my dad's garage so nobody throws all these neat items out. We should really get going, it's almost five thirty." So they grabbed the bikes and paired up and pedaled down the street across town. As they pedaled across town, Jason noticed his uncle Jimmy, who worked for the local sanitation company, and he waved at him. Jason yelled back at Bobby while he's peddling his bike, "I should ask my uncle if we could one day walk through the dump site. I bet we'd find some real neat stuff!"

"Yeah, Jason," Bobby replied, "I'll ask him."

Jason replied, "I sure will, tomorrow he's coming to Mom's for dinner." So they bicycled to the fork in the town, and they waved to Jody and Sarah as they split down the other fork of the neighborhood.

"See you tomorrow at school," Bobby yelled to the girls.

"Okay." Giggles were coming from the girls. So Bobby finally got to Jason's house and dropped him off.

Jason said, "Okay, Bobby, I'll hide this in my dad's garage. I'll label the box 'The Golden Box' on it. I'll see you tomorrow." Bobby rushed home, and as he's riding by an old two-story house that looked abandoned, he noticed a light on in one of the rooms upstairs. Weird, he thought to himself. "So creepy," he mumbled.

The next day came; at 7:15 a.m., the school bus stopped at Sarah's house first, then Jody's, then Jason's, and finally, Bobby's house, which was located a little bit farther than the rest lived, which was the farthest from school. Sometimes, Bobby would ride his bike to school, but lately, they all had been riding the bus so that they could chat before school—always about interesting stuff they had found or funny stuff that they saw. They all got along so well, they would laugh and poke fun at each other all the time. They all had most of their classes together but two, and at many times, they passed notes in class, especially if a movie was being shown by a teacher. So the bus came to a stop at the front of the school called Kalamazoo Town School. The kids piled up to get on the bus in a single file like little soldiers. The last on the bus usually were the four friends.

Their first class together was English with Ms. White. She was such an attractive lady, tall, and had a slender build. She always wore such beautiful dresses. Her hair looked gold, had curled bangs, and was styled loosely to her shoulders. She only put on stylish glasses when she read from her book. She wore bright-red lipstick. Many kids would leave an apple or a drawing on her desk. She was everybody's favorite teacher because she was so pretty and nice and always wanted to help if you didn't understand. The bell rang, and she pulled the classroom door closed. She walked over to her desk and said, "Attention, class." She tapped the chalkboard with her pointer, and everybody would stop talking. She said, "For this weekend, starting tomorrow, your assignment is to write two pages and draw a picture of the most interesting event that took place in the last few months." Jody looked back at Sarah and said, "Do you know what you're writing about, Sarah?"

Bobby told Sarah, "Oh, I know!"

Jason and Jody blurted out, "I don't know yet. Let's all meet Saturday and figure it all out." They all smiled at each other and nodded in agreement.

They all went to their classes after Ms. White and then met up at lunchtime. For some reason, Jody always brought her lunch in a lunch pail, and so did Sarah. The boys always got their lunch at the cafeteria; often, they would trade each other items from their lunch and talk about what they were going to do for the weekend. Jason blurted out, "Oh, my uncle Jimmy is coming over for dinner tonight."

"Is it already Friday?" Bobby mumbled.

"I'll ask if we all can go to the dump yard and walk around to find some neat stuff for our 'golden box.' We can walk around for a little bit while the yard is closed."

"That would be so exciting!" Jody and Bobby said.

Sarah said softly, "I don't know if I could go, my parents are both home during the weekend."

"Well, you don't have to tell them exactly what we're doing," they all said.

Jason said, "We'll just meet like we do on Wednesdays and shoot by real quick, and nobody will know." The bell rang, and lunch break was over, and they all went their separate ways to class.

* * *

The bell rang three times, which meant that 2:45 p.m. came along, and school was over. They all met up at the front of the school to take the bus home. Jason's dad was waiting at the front of the school in the coolest black convertible Cadillac car that they had ever seen. Jason's dad picked him up to take Jason back to the deli his dad owned so that he could work at the deli for a few hours, stocking the shelves and freezer. The deli was called Papa Joe's Deli and Market. Most of the locals would purchase their meat and sausages there. It smelled so good in there, like you could eat everything up in one visit. On Fridays after school, all four would meet up at the deli to share a salami and pastrami cheese sandwich; it was to die for. They didn't have to pay, Jason would always say, "Poppa has us covered guys!"

"Thanks, Poppa," they all would say. "He even gave us our own soda pops." What a great treat that was!

So supper came at the Ferrahis', and Jason could hardly wait; his uncle Jimmy was coming over. He was so excited to talk to him. Jimmy was such a macho guy; he was built like a weightlifter— shoulders were like Popeye the Sailor Man, and he had a big jet black mustache. He had jet-black hair where he slicked it all back like Elvis and made a pompadour with a ducktail. He smelled like he took a bath in his cologne and wore lots of gold. Whenever he came over, he'd always kiss my dad's cheeks as my dad would do him or the family. He'd kiss Jason's mama's hand and cheeks and whirl her around in a slow swirl; it always made her laugh and smile. He'd pick us kids up and throw us over his shoulder one at a time then slam us softly down on the couch and tickle us all crazy. Since Jason was older, he stopped doing that and just roughed him up and made Jason put his dukes up, and he'd throw punches at him, telling him to block his face, and then he'd give him a knucklehead rub then kiss his forehead. He'd always ask how he was doing in school, then he'd ramble on about, "Stay in school," with a thick Italian accent.

Jason would reply, "I know, Uncle Jimmy, I know," then he'd whisper in his ear, "Are you dating any hot girls?"

He'd laugh and say, "Not yet, Uncle, not yet."

He'd say, "Ahhhh, you have enough time, you're a good-looking guy! You keep your mind on school then the girls, ha ha ha," he'd laugh so loud. Then he and Pops would go out to the garage located at the back. His little brother Richie, age seven; his little baby sister Lani, age four; and Jason were never allowed to go out there. Jason would always wonder what they were talking about. He'd ask his ma, and she'd never tell him, except, "You don't need to go out there. Papa is talking business out there. It's not a place for kids." Gosh, he could hardly wait to talk to Uncle Jimmy. Jason just wanted to eat already and then, between dessert, talk to him. Finally, Ma said, "Supper is ready! Go knock on the garage door and tell Papa that dinner is ready." Jason raced out there like he was sprinting for his life. He then ran inside, washed his hands, and sat at the dining table and waited for everybody to sit to eat supper. His pops and uncle came in, washed their hands, and sat down at the table. He watched where Jimmy sat, then he scooted right next to him. He patted Jason's head and smiled. Then his brother sat next to him. Jason's mama set all the dishes down on the table then sat across from them while his baby sister sat next to him. Dinner was all adult talk. The kids were to be seen and not heard at the table, so they didn't say a word unless spoken to. Supper was so delicious. Ma made a pecan pie for dessert. After supper, they all went into the living room and sat on the couches around a marble coffee table. Pa always sat in his Italian brown leather lounger chair. It sat deep and super soft and comfortable with arms at its side. Jason's pa would always set his feet up on the matching leather ottoman and smoke a cigar and looked at the paper under an overhanging brass lamp. Ma brought a slice of pie to each of them about thirty minutes after supper. When Pa got up to use the restroom, Jason whispered to his uncle Jimmy, "Uncle Jimmy, can I ask you for a favor?"

He said, "Sure, kiddo."

"Me and three of my best friends are searching for treasures for a class assignment, and we were wondering if you would take us and let us walk through the dump yard to find some unique pieces while the dump is closed?"

He replied, "Oh, well, um, okay, sure! Come Saturday around ten thirty, I have to go do a few things there, I'll be the only one there."

"That's great, Uncle Jimmy, you're the best," Jason told him.

Then Pops came back into the room, and they changed the subject to cars. After he ate his pie, Jason gave his uncle a kiss on the cheeks and a hug and then ran off to his bedroom. As he's running down the hall to his room, he yelled out, "Thank you, Mama, for a delicious supper!" then he ran back and gave her a hug and a kiss. He couldn't wait to tell his friends the next day at school. He wished he had a way to tell them now.

Jason whispered out loud to himself, "I'll go to bed and get up early to be ready for Bobby." They rode their bikes on Fridays to school so they could go to Papa's for a sandwich after school.

CHAPTER 2

The next morning came. Jason got up early and got ready for school. Bobby got to Jason's house at 7:30 a.m. They ate a bowl of cereal and toast then left to meet up at Jody's house. On the way, Jason told

Bobby the great news that Uncle Jimmy said yes to them going to the dump where he worked and let them walk through to find some new items for the golden box. They were so excited to tell the girls; all they could talk about was what they were going to find. Bobby pedaled his bike so fast to Jody's house that Jason almost fell off the handlebars. Bobby mentioned that when he was coming over this morning, he saw something strange at the old two-story house that looked abandoned on the corner of Wilks and Fifth. Bobby saw someone standing and looking out the window upstairs. It looked like an old lady, scary-looking with long hair and a big nose. Jason replied, "Really? Gosh, that sounds creepy, Bobby. Maybe after we go to the dump, we can swing by there and check it out closer?"

Bobby said, "Yeah, let's do that!"

They finally arrived at Jody's house. Sarah and Jody were sitting on the porch with their lunch boxes. Jason blurted out, "Oh my gosh, girls, I had supper last night with my uncle Jimmy, and I asked him about going through the dump, and he said yes we could."

The girls were so happy, they were like, "Really? that's great! What time and where do we meet?"

Jason said, "Okay, we will meet at the clock tower at the town square, then we will ride our bikes down the way toward the river dock, then Uncle Jimmy will pick us up at 10:30 a.m. in his red hot rod 1936 Ford pickup truck and will take us the rest of the way into the dump."

"Sounds perfect!" Bobby and Jody replied.

Sarah said out loud, "I wanna go, but I'm not sure if my parents will let me leave the house to meet you guys. If you don't see me at the clock tower at 10:10 a.m., then my parents didn't let me leave to go meet you guys." Her face looked sad after saying that.

"It's okay, Sarah," Jody said. "If you don't get to go, we'll still meet at school on Monday to tell you what we found."

"Okay," Sarah replied and smiled. They both pedaled down the streets and came to the school front, parked the bicycles in the bike rack, then walked to class. Friday was a fun day at school. Usually, in

Ms. White's class, she would play a fun movie, which would take up most of the class time. Sometimes, she'd bake cookies or snacks to pass around during the movie. Today, she said good morning and asked for them to hand in their homework issued to them on Monday on learning the difference between nouns and pronouns. The homework had twenty-five questions. Then she made a speech about a field trip next month and that she would need $10 from each student and their parents' signature to go out of town on the bus. The field trip was going to be at the famous Coca-Cola manufacturer. After that, she reminded us about the writing assignment and said we were going to watch a short film. After that, she handed out the forms to be filled out by the parents, then she set up the movie player, turned out the lights, then started the film. The film was a cartoon of Popeye the Sailor Man and Olive. It was so great that Bobby's face lit up like a Christmas tree. After class, they went to their other classes then met up for lunch at the cafeteria. Jody and Sarah met at a table and waited for the boys outside. Bobby and Jason met at the lunch line and got their lunch special: pizza, french fries, salad, and a pudding cup. When they met the girls, they were all talking about the field trip with Ms. White. "Oh, we can't wait!" they all said. The conversation between them circled around like a tornado about the paper that's due, the field trip, Saturday dump trip, and the new kid that moved in down across the street from Bobby on Thursday. Bobby said, "With the heavy breath, the new kid looks kind of nerdy."

Sarah said, "What do you mean, Bobby?"

Bobby replied, "Well he's super skinny-brown hair combed back and over to the side." Bobby mentioned that he thought he saw that he had a bicycle, but not for sure. "I'll keep an eye on him to see what his story is about."

Jason said, "Maybe we should invite him to the ball field on Wednesday."

"Nah," Bobby said, "why? Four is enough in our club, isn't it?"

Jody said, "If he's nice, perhaps we should invite him." Sarah agreed! Well, then, in the middle of that conversation, the bell rang to end lunch.

Jason added, "Are we gonna meet up after class and go to my pop's for a sandwich and some soda pop?"

"We sure are," they all answered. "See you later! Bye!" They all waved and walked to their classes. While Bobby and Jason were walking down the hall, a big, tall jockey kid ran into Bobby and said, "*Watch* it, dummy!"

Bobby said, "*You watch* it!" and out of the blue, the jock hauled off and socked Bobby in the face, hitting his eye. Bobby fell back and knocked over the garbage cans.

Jason yelled out, "Pick on someone your own size," and rushed to Bobby's side. "Are you okay, Bob?" He helped him up and walked him down to the principal's office where the nurse's clinic was located.

As Bobby held his eye, he told the secretary at the front desk that somebody hit him in the face, and he needed to see the nurse. She replied, "When did this happen, and who did this, Bobby?"

He muffled back, "I dunno who it was, some big guy."

She then said, "You're going to have to talk to the vice principal about this after you see the nurse, and your parents are going to have to be notified." Bobby replied with a sad okay.

Next, Bobby went to lie down at the nurse's office with an ice pack on his eye. Bobby's eye started to swell up and turned all blackand-blue with blood at the corner of the white of his eye. Jason ran down the hall and saw Jody and told her what had happened. "Please tell Sarah," Jason told her.

"I will," Jody said! Then Jason ran to his class to make sure he wasn't late. He watched the clock minute by minute, and it was only 2:00 p.m. "One more class, then we're off for the weekend." Two forty-five in the afternoon came, and the bell rang three times; school was then out for the weekend. Jason ran to meet up with Jody and Sarah. They looked for Bobby. They went to the office and asked about Bobby.

The secretary at the front desk replied that Bobby's mom came to pick him up, so they walked to the bike rack to see if Bobby's bike was still there; it sure was. So Jason got the bike and told the girls to follow him to his papa's deli for a snack. They giggled and said, *"Sure!"* They rode through the town and to the deli. Papa had a sandwich already made and cut into fours. Jason spoke to his pa and said that Bobby got hit in the eye, so he won't be eating with them today. His dad said, "Who hit him, and *why?*"

Jason replied, "Not sure why the guy hit Bobby, he was mean and big."

"Well, that isn't right," Papa said, "should I find out?"

Jason said, "No, Papa, it's okay. I'm sure it was just an accident."

"Well, let me know if there are any more problems. More than likely, I serve meat to his parents or family, so I will handle it!"

"Thanks, Pa, it's okay right now," Jason replied. Jason and the girls enjoyed the sandwich with a soda pop of their choice. Sarah had a 10, 2, 4 Dr. Pepper; Jody and Jason had a Coca-Cola. They were glass bottles with a metal cap served extra cold. When Uncle Sam, who worked behind the counter with Pa, he'd opened the soda pop bottle caps, and it fizzed out so loud that it made their mouths water. Next, they saw Bobby walk in with his mom. They all yelled, "Bobby! Are you okay?" He had a black eye that was all swollen.

"Yeah, I'm okay!" Bobby replied. "It's just a little sore."

"Want your half of the sandwich?"

"Yeah, sure! Let me tell my mom first."

Bobby went to his mom and asked, and she said, "Sure," that he could join his friends. "Bring your bicycle home, Bobby," his mom told him. Bobby rushed back over to his friends and started eating half of the sandwich. Uncle Sammy asked what kind of pop he wanted, and he replied, "10-2-4, Uncle Sammy. Thanks a lot!" So the four sat and enjoyed their sandwich and pop and talked about Bobby's black eye and the trip to the dump and how fun it was going to be. After they were done, the girls took off on their way. "We'll see you tomorrow at 10:00 a.m. at the clock tower at the town square," Jody said.

Bobby and Jason replied, "Okay, see you then!" Then Jason and Bobby went their way, but before they went home, they rode by the creepy old two-story house on Wilks and Fifth to see if they could see something new. When they got to the corner, they saw three old ladies sitting on the porch table and chairs. The house looked so spooky and dark. All the trees and bushes were overgrown. They sat at a distance on Bobby's bike to see what was going on. The old ladies had so many cats hanging around but no dogs. Bobby said to Jason, "Do you see what I see, Jason?" Jason replied, "Yeah, what's going on there? I thought this house was abandoned? Some of the windows are boarded up. If someone was living in it, wouldn't you think that all the windows would be open?" in a slow uncomfortable voice.

Bobby said, "Let's go before they notice us." So they took off down the street. Bobby dropped off Jason at his house then rode slowly back to his house, passing the house on Wilks and Fifth. As he passed the house, he only noticed one old lady. She noticed him and pointed her finger at him. He looked around as if she was pointing to someone else, but she was for sure pointing at him. She was dressed in a long-type dress, dark in color, and no print. Her hair was black, straight, and long. Bobby thought to himself, *Why the heck is she pointing at me? I didn't do anything.* So Bobby pedaled his bike fast the rest of the way home. When Bobby got home, he asked his mom about the creepy house, and she replied, "I believe it's empty, son."

Bobby replied, "No, Mom, I think people live there. I saw three old ladies there and cats, lots of them!"

His mom laughed. "Oh, Bobby, you're silly." The evening grew later and later but seemed to creep along. All the kids were so anxious to go with Jason's uncle on Saturday morning, they could hardly sleep.

CHAPTER 3

Saturday morning, 8:30 a.m., came. They had all put their alarm clocks on. They ate some breakfast and put on their playclothes. They had all told their parents they were doing some research for an assignment that Ms. White gave them on Wednesday and that they were going to meet at the school baseball field. Surprisingly, Sarah's parents allowed her to go as well, so they all met at the clock tower at 10:00 a.m. sharp. The downtown area wasn't very far from all of their houses—all walking distance. They hopped on their bikes and rode down to the road that headed toward the river dock and waited for Uncle Jimmy. Shortly thereafter, they saw Uncle Jimmy pull around the way in his red truck. He stopped, and they hid their bikes in the brush then piled into the back of the truck and held on. It was a dirt road that Uncle Jimmy took, a bumpy ride to say the least. They came to a gate where Jimmy stopped the truck and got out and unlocked a chain wrapped around the handle. He got back in the truck and pulled forward a bit, then yelled out the window, "You got the gate, boys?" Bobby and Jason hopped out and pulled the gate shut and locked it then hopped back in the truck. Uncle Jimmy then started the rest of the journey down the road, which had a slight downward slope. You could tell that they were at the dump just by the smell. It was horrible and kind of sour smelling.

The girls had their sweatshirt over their noses and were saying how gross it smelled. The boys said, "Ahhhh, it's not that bad." Soon, Uncle Jimmy pulled to an office-looking building just below a huge machine. When Jason asked what that machine was, Jimmy replied, "It's a crane." One of them had a huge magnet on one, and the other had a clawlike scoop on one. Off to a short distance, there were two bulldozers and a tractor.

"Wow! It looks like it's fun to work there," Bobby mumbled to Jason.

Uncle Jimmy said, "Okay, kids, you have one hour, make sure you don't cut yourself, fall, or get lost."

They all replied in one answer, "Okay, Uncle Jimmy!" Off they went walking slowly. Right away, Bobby found a stick to poke at things. He twirled it around like a sword then said, "I'll use this to lift things to look under."

Jason said, "Uncle Jimmy mentioned that around to the right of this mound are household items instead of garbage items," so they headed around the mound. When they got around the mound, their eyes got all big and said, "*Wow*! Look at all the stuff! It's piled so high!" It was like a huge yard sale, like tons of houses were picked up and dumped out—couches, tables, toys, garden tools. "Most of the stuff look in good shape, why would people throw these items out?" Sarah mentioned. So they started picking through things. They slightly started to drift apart while searching for the coolest items to put in the gold box.

Right away, Bobby yelled, "Oh my gosh, I just found a pocket watch."

Sarah said, "Look at this necklace. It has ruby and black jewels." She quickly put it in the paper bag that she brought. Jody screamed! And right when they all looked, a little stray cat hopped out and ran away. Time was going by fast as they looked through the treasures. Jason yelled out, "It's almost time to head back, guys." They continued to search for another ten minutes. Uncle Jimmy honked his horn to tell them to head back. They had gathered a few items each in their paper bags and started to head back to the office where Uncle Jimmy was. When they got there, Uncle Jimmy said, "Did you guys find some good stuff?"

"We sure did," they all replied! With their bags in their arms, they hopped in the back of his truck and waited for him to come. He locked up the office and got in the truck and started up the hill back up to the gate, which he unlocked and swung open. He got back in the truck and then stopped shortly ahead. He said, "Okay, boys, you know what you gotta do." Bobby and Jason hopped out then shut and locked the gate and hopped back into the truck. Jimmy drove back to where they hid their bikes and let them all out.

"We all appreciate you letting us look through the dump, Uncle Jimmy. You're the best!"

"See you later, guys!"

"Thanks, Uncle!" Jason yelled! They hopped on their bikes with their paper bags filled with stuff and headed back to the clock tower. "Oh, darn," Jason mumbled, "I forgot to bring the box from my dad's garage. I wonder if I can sneak back home without being seen and pick it up so we can show what we all found at the dump today."

"Yeah," Bobby said. "Okay, so you girls hold this stuff, *don't* look, and we'll go to Jason's house and get the box. See you right back here in like ten minutes." Jason and Bobby pedaled quickly back to the garage. They slipped at the back into the garage, got the box, then pedaled back to meet the girls. They joined the girls and then rode over to the ballpark to find out what each other found, so they reached into their paper bags and pulled out one item.

"You go first, Sarah," Bobby said. Sarah reached in and pulled out her treasure, and it was a long antique-looking necklace with ruby and black jewels. It was dirty but beautiful. The only thing wrong with the necklace was the fastening clasp. Everybody said "wow" upon seeing the item. Sarah added, "I can take it home and wash it really well and then bring it back and put it in the box!"

"Good idea," Jody expressed. Then Bobby pulled out his treasure from his bag, and it was a pocket watch—silver and gold, but it was missing the faceplate and the chain. "That's so cool," everybody said. Jody reached into her bag and pulled a silver-plated antique mirror with a handle. The mirror was cracked across it all the way, but it was beautiful, to say the least. Next was Jason's find. He reached into his bag and pulled out a small clock. The clock looked like a cuckoo clock made out of wood. It was detailed slightly and had a little drawer under the actual clock. Everybody said, "Wow! That's way cool. Does the drawer pull out?"

Jason said, "I don't think so." He tried pulling on it, but it didn't budge. "Maybe it's just for looks," Jason said.

"*Wow*, everybody, I would say that we struck gold," Jody said broadly.

"So let's all put our stuff in and bring it back out on Wednesday."

Bobby added, "I think I wanna take my pocket watch home to clean it."

Sarah said, "Yeah, me too, I'd like to take the necklace home and clean it."

Jody said, "Yeah, I can take mine home and polish it to a nice shine."

"Well, okay," Jason added, "I'll take the clock home and wax it to a shine, wind the clock, and see if it works right." So they closed the box up and put their items back into their bags, hopped on their bikes, and started riding home. When they were riding through the town, they saw the new kid with his mom and sister at the local market. He noticed them and then looked away. "Wonder if Monday he'll be coming to school?" Jody asked.

"Hope so," Sarah said.

Jason and Bobby grumbled and said, "Yeah, we'll see."

Jody said in a high-pitched voice, "You guys are so stupid. He looks very nice but shy. If you guys don't go say hi and find his name out, I will." Jody and Sarah started laughing like little chicken hens.

Bobby was all, "Whatever, girls," so they went their separate ways. It was time for lunch. The girls took their items right into their room, and Bobby and Jason took a little detour first before heading home. They decided to stop by the creepy old house on Wilks and Fifth. When they rode up, they rode up on the sidewalk that attached to their front yard. They walked slowly next to the fence with the overgrown bushes and trees. Four cats came out of the front gate and started to meow like they were hungry. Jason whispered forcefully, "Shoo, cats, shoo!" Then all of a sudden, one of the old ladies opened the gate and said, "*Hey!* Don't kick my cats!"

Bobby mumbled, "No, ma'am, we didn't kick at your cats, we were just walking by."

The old lady was mumbling under her breath something they couldn't understand. They tried to quickly walk past her, but she moved her rake in their path. They both said, "Excuse me, ma'am, excuse us!" They finally got past her, and by that time, there were at least ten cats circling around them.

Bobby said, "Did you hear her say something about a clock or watch?"

Jason replied, "I'm not sure. She was saying something over and over." They quickly hopped on the bike and drove fast back home.

CHAPTER 4

The kids all got back home, and each and every one pulled out their item and started cleaning and shining the treasures they found. Strangely, they all found almost perfect items that could be cleaned up and be kept. Bobby showed his dad his pocket watch and asked if it would cost a lot to get a faceplate. Bobby's dad replied, "I don't think so, I'll ask around for you, Bob, it sure is a nice watch."

"Thanks, Dad, I really like it," Bobby said. While Bobby was looking at the watch, he noticed an engraving on the back: GS. He wondered who the watch used to belong to. He couldn't wait to tell the rest of them.

At Jason's, he went to the garage and looked for some wax to shine the clock. He found some on the shelf above his dad's workbench. He started by wiping it all down with a damp cloth then started waxing it from top to bottom. Jason noticed on the bottom of the clock that it had an engraving: GS. Jason thought to himself, *I wonder who it used to belong to.* Jason tried to open the little drawer on the bottom, but it seemed to be stuck or not a full drawer. So Jason got a screwdriver and tried prying it open. He got excited when he saw that it was a drawer, just stuck on something. Jason took his fingers and slowly tried to reach in, and he felt something. While fishing around tightly in the drawer with his fingers, Jason was successful and opened it. The items inside the drawer were an ace card, a dice, and a black rock. The black rock was shiny. He thought to himself, *That's so strange.* He wondered why there were those items in there, so he put them back and continued to wax and wound the clock. "Oh my gosh," Jason yelled out, "it works! It works!" Jason couldn't wait to tell the rest of the crew about it. His mom came in and noticed the clock. She asked him sternly, "Where did you get that clock, Jason?"

Jason replied, "Mama, I found it outside a garbage by the river dock," he continued, "it was so dirty that I brought it home and cleaned it up."

Jason's mom asked, "Are you sure that's where you got it because if you didn't, you're going to have to give it back!"

Jason pleaded, "No, Mama, it was in the garbage when Bobby, Jody, Sarah, and I hung out earlier. We tried to find items that we call treasures to clean up and talk about."

Jason's mom said "Okay" and turned around and walked out of his room. Jason sighed with relief.

Sarah took the necklace home and soaked it in dish soap for a little bit. When she pulled it out and dried it, she noticed that on the back of the necklace, there was an engraving that had the initials VS. Sarah wondered who once owned the beautiful necklace. She couldn't wait to tell the rest of the guys.

Jody took the silver mirror and soaked it in warm soapy water then asked her grandma if she knew how to shine the mirror that she found outside a garbage can. Her grandma walked to the kitchen and pulled out from under the sink a small metal container that had a silver-cleaning compound in it. She pulled out a white small rag and told her to dab a little on the rag and, in a circular motion, rub the mirror then take the clean part of the rag and rub it over. It should shine right up. As she rubbed the mirror, and the dark smoky black soot started going away, she noticed an engraving on the mirror; it was the letters *V* and *S*. *Wow,* she thought, *I wonder who owned this before. It's so gorgeous.* She went to show her grandma, who was sitting in the living room crocheting another blanket. "Look, Grandma," Jody said softly. "Isn't it beautiful?"

Her grandma replied, "Yes, dear, it really is beautiful."

"Look, it has an engraving, did you know anybody that had those initials?" Jody asked. Her grandma answered, "No, I don't believe I do, sorry, dear."

"Oh, right, well, I'm gonna go lie down in my room."

So through the weekend, each of them had cleaned and polished their findings then set it up either on their desk or dresser. They couldn't wait to see each other so they could tell the others that their items had engravings.

CHAPTER 5

So the weekend came and gone. Monday morning came, and the kids woke. They all decided to take the bus so they could sit and chat with each other before class. Sarah and Jody first caught the bus. Each of them said that they cleaned their items and found an engraving. They both asked at the same time what initials were engraved. They both answered *VS*.

"What?" they said loudly.

"Oh my god, our items have the same initials. I wonder if Bobby's and Jason's do as well."

Jason hopped on the bus and headed straight to the back of the bus where Jody and Sarah were sitting. He asked them how everything was going. The girls couldn't wait to tell him their exciting news. They blurted out, "Our items have the same engraving!"

"What?" Jason replied. "That's so neat! Funny, mine has one on the bottom of my clock, it's *GS* though."

Soon, the bus pulled up to Bobby's pickup sight, and they saw Bobby with his black eye and books. He jumped on the bus and rushed to the back.

"Oh my gosh, guys, when I cleaned my watch, I found it had an engraving on the bottom." They asked Bobby what it was. Bobby replied, "GS."

Jason said, "Buddy, oh my gosh, that's what my clock has on the bottom, and Jody's and Sarah's have *VS*. I wonder whose items these used to be? We have to find out, we just got to, guys." Soon, they pulled up to the front of the school. They gathered their books and items and walked off the bus and to their class. Ms. White greeted the class cheerfully. She asked if everybody had a good weekend and if there was anything that anybody wanted to share. The four looked at each other as if they wanted to say something but decided to write about it. Then she asked if anybody had the field trip signatures from their parents. Only a few had them. She added to make sure and have them signed by the end of the month. She then said in a higher-pitch voice, "Okay, class, I have a twenty-question quiz for you." The whole class seemed to have moaned with disappointment. She said, "Oh, class, it's okay. This quiz is for me to see if you need more teaching in a certain area. The quiz is only a half point, so try your best. Leave the papers facedown, and when I tell you, you can flip them over." She passed them all out and then went to her desk and watched the clock hand, and then she spoke out, *"Are* you ready? Okay, turn your papers over, you have twenty minutes."

When Jody turned the quiz over, she smiled and looked back at Jason and nodded. "Easy!" Jody looked over at Bobby, and he seemed to be having trouble. Sarah was fully concentrated on her test. On the last two questions, it asked what color were the shoes she wore on Friday and what would be a good Friday event to do if they could choose. *I love Ms. White*, Jody thought to herself. Jody finished the English questions and the two fun questions and flipped it over first. The rest of the class followed, but Bobby seemed to be having some trouble. Then Ms. White yelled out, "Okay, class, time's up. Turn your papers over, I will collect." Bobby scurried to finish the last two questions. Ms. White picked up the papers and went to her desk and then asked that they all open their books and read pages 96–116. Ms. White went over the quiz and graded it. Time came to the end of class, and she mentioned that Friday would be a test on pages 96–196 and asked them to make sure to read it well. The bell rang to switch classes. Everyone filed out of the class like cattle walking through, but Ms. White called Bobby back to her desk and asked what was wrong and why he only answered half of the questions. He mumbled, "I dunno." She said in a soft-spoken voice, "It's okay, Bobby, if you need extra help, I am always here. I noticed that you switched your letters in a few answers." He questioned where. She then told Bobby, "You tell me where." Bobby looked over it and couldn't find the mistake. Ms. White pointed out his mistakes and then circled them and said, "I'd like for you to take a little test in the library tomorrow, Bobby. It won't be worth any points for the class, this is just for you and me to see where there are some problems." She finished up by saying, "You're a good student, I'll help you as much as you need, don't get so upset, it's gonna be okay." Bobby's face turned from sadness to smiles quickly. He grabbed his stuff and quickly walked to his other classes. Ms. White called over to Bobby's other classes to talk to each teacher to ask if they noticed Bobby having trouble with any grammar. She wrote down that a few teachers noticed some issues. She gathered all her papers and made a note to have Bobby take a dyslexic test tomorrow.

The lunch bell rang. The crew got their lunches together and went and sat at a bench. Bobby seemed very upset and quiet. They all asked him why, and he replied, "Nothing." Jody was sitting next to him and gave him a side hug and pat. "It's gonna be okay, Bobby. My older sister had reading and grammar problems but got help and has done well in school."

Bobby then opened up and said, "Yeah, Ms. White wants to give me a test tomorrow, so we'll see what she thinks."

Then Sarah said, "Did you guys answer the last question about her shoes and what would be a fun Friday event? I answered black high heels."

Jody said, "Yeah, I answered blue high heels."

Jason said, "I guessed with black."

Bobby blurted out, "They were brown, folks. *Brown!*"

They all turned and said, "What?"

He replied, "Yes, she had brown shoes on to match her brown skirt."

They all started laughing. "That's so funny, Bobby. We shall see what is the right answer. What did you guys put that would be a fun event to do on Friday?"

Jason said, "To play soccer during class."

Jody said, "We should do crafts."

Bobby said, "We should bring different desserts and watch a movie during class like *Godzilla*."

Sarah ended with, "I think our Friday should have a magic show with a magician and eat popcorn and punch. I know a magician, he's my mom's brother's cousin. I'll ask my mom to see if he will do a magic show for our class."

"That would be amazing," Jody, Bobby, and Jason said.

The lunch bell rang, and they all gathered their garbage and threw it away and walked to their classes. So school went on, the kids went to the rest of their classes, and the bell rang at two forty-five. School's out! The kids seemed to be full of energy, hopping around like an egg being fried in a frying pan. They all filed onto the bus. The four, of course, went to the back of the bus to chat about stuff. When they all got dropped off, they all said, "See you tomorrow." Bobby went home and had to tell his mom and dad that Ms. White was giving him a test tomorrow. He really didn't want to tell them he was having problems because both of his parents were teachers for college, so Bobby went straight to his room to lay on his bed. He threw his baseball up in the air, hitting the ceiling. His mom heard the thumps from the ball hitting the ceiling and came to his room and said, "What's wrong, *Bobby*?"

Bobby replied, "Nothing, Mom," followed by a big sigh.

His mom walked closer then sat on the end of the bed and said, "I can tell there is something bothering you, Bobby."

He sat up and asked, "Mom, am I dumb?"

Bobby's mom was shocked at what came out of his mouth. She replied, "Bobby, I never want to hear you say that again. Of course not, you're not dumb! What's wrong, son?"

Bobby started crying and said, "Ms. White wants to give me a test tomorrow. Only me!"

His mom asked, "Why? What is the test about?"

He answered. "I'm not sure, Mom. I always have problems writing, and we had a quiz today, and I struggled with it."

"How, dear?"

"Ms. White pointed out that I switched my letters," Bobby added.

"Did you misspell them, Bobby?"

"No, not really, Mom. She said that a lot of my words were backward. I don't know what that means."

His mom reached over and gave him hugs. "I'll call Ms. White tomorrow and find out exactly what's going on. You'll be okay, Bobby! You should change your school clothes and go outside and have some fun. Throw your ball or even go introduce yourself to the new kid across the street."

Bobby changed his clothes and took his mitt and ball outside to throw and catch. When he went outside, he noticed the new neighbor kid playing basketball in his driveway, so he watched him for a bit but tried to act like he wasn't watching. Well, a few minutes went by, and the new kid's ball rolled over to Bobby's yard. Bobby stopped the ball, picked it up, and started bouncing the ball back toward the new kid. The new kid came running after it and said, "Hey, thanks! Sorry about that."

Bobby replied, "No problem. I like your basketball net, did your dad just put it up above the garage door?"

The new kid said, "Yeah, it's super fun to play. Do you play?"

Bobby replied, "Not much, I don't have a basketball net or ball."

The new kid quickly answered, "Hey, would you like to play ball with me?"

Bobby said enthusiastically, "*Sure!*"

Bobby then added, "Hey, my name is Bobby, what's yours?"

"Oh, nice to meet you, Bobby. My name is Adam. Nice, let's play some ball, Bobby," Adam shouted. The boys seemed to hit it off quickly, taking turns throwing the basketball. As they played outside, Bobby mentioned, "I saw that you have a bicycle, is it yours or someone else's?"

Adam answered, "Oh yeah, it's mine. I love riding my bike. Do you have one, Bobby?"

Bobby answered, "Yeah, I have one, it's a Schwinn with a paper rack at the back.

"Oh! Do you throw paper, Bobby?" Adam asked.

Bobby answered, "Nah, next summer though. I want to make some extra cash to collect some comic books."

"Oh yeah," Adam asked, "I have tons of comic books, wanna see?" So they tossed the basketball to the side of the driveway and ran inside. Adam's house was two-story, white in color, and had a brick front and a wooden shake roof. When they ran inside, their face was slammed with the best-smelling pie or cookies that they had ever smelled.

"Oh my gosh, Adam, it smells so great in here."

He stopped in his tracks and said, "Oh yeah, here, let me introduce you to my mom. She loves baking stuff."

"Okay," Bobby said. So they both walked into the kitchen, and Adam's mom was standing by the kitchen sink.

"Hi, Adam, it looks like you made a new friend, who might this be?" Adam's mother asked.

Bobby held out his hand and said, "Pleased to meet you, ma'am, my name is Bobby Schutzers. I live across the street."

She extended her petite hand and grabbed Bobby's and said, "Well, pleased to meet you, Bobby. My name is Mrs. Garcia." Bobby's face turned red from shyness and embarrassment. Mrs. Garcia was such a beautiful lady. She seemed to have legs for days. She was in a red checkered dress with a white-and-red apron on. Her eyes were piercing green with a dark silky-straight hair pulled back in a clip. Bobby's mouth opened while he stared at Mrs. Garcia as she spoke. It was obvious that Bobby was taken by her sweet voice and kind, gentle beauty.

"What are you and Bobby up to?"

Adam and Bobby answered quickly, "Just playing ball." Adam then mentioned that he was going to show Bobby his comic books.

She replied, "Oh, that's nice, Adam, but would you boys like to have a few cookies and some milk first?"

"*Sure!*" Bobby blurted out. "I love fresh cookies." His enthusiasm made Mrs. Garcia giggle under her breath. She got two white china saucer plates and a spatula and scooped out two cookies each then opened the cabinet and got two small juice glasses and poured them some milk.

"Go ahead and sit at the table and eat and drink this before you go up to your bedroom, Adam and Bobby." They both could barely talk; they gobbled their cookies down and gulped their milk. After they finished, they thanked Mrs. Garcia and then ran upstairs. Mrs. Garcia smiled as she washed the plates and yelled, "Don't run in the house, Adam."

"Okay, Mom," Adam yelled down from upstairs. Adam dived under his bed and pulled out a hatbox. He set it up on the bed between Bobby and him. It was heavy because Adam grunted while lifting it onto the bed. He then unstrapped the straps on the hatbox to open the lid. He opened the box, and on top was a Superman comic. It had its plastic cover still on. It was like Adam opened up a box that had shiny gold in it.

Bobby's jaw slid open in ah. He then said, "Oh my gosh, Adam! Where did you get these?"

"Ah, I got them as gifts and my dad."

"*Wow!*" Bobby exclaimed, "they're beautiful, they're in mint condition. Do you ever read them, Adam?"

"Yeah." Adam chuckled. "Of course, I do. I just take really great care of them. I look at them one at a time and then put the plastic back on them and keep them in this hatbox my dad gave me."

"Oh my gosh, I can't wait to tell the crew!" Bobby yelled out.

Adam said, "Crew. Who's the crew?"

"Oh, you'll meet them. *My* friends, my best friend Jason. Yeah, his dad owns the local deli called Papa Joe's Deli."

"Oh yeah, I did see that, my mom went there this weekend."

"Yeah," Bobby said, "and my other two friends Sarah and Jody."

"Whoa!" Adam said. "Girls? You have two friends that are girls?"

Bobby said, "Yeah, they're supercool."

"Oh really? I think I might have seen you all together on bikes the other day."

"Oh yeah, we saw you."

"Yea, that's them, but Jody is the only one that has a bike. Sarah doesn't have one yet."

"Oh," Adam said. "Check out the Archie comic, it's so funny. I love Archie."

"Do you mind if I borrow two or three to look at tonight? I promise to take extra care of them!"

"Okay, sure," Adam replied.

Bobby asked Adam, "Are you going to start school tomorrow?"

Adam answered, "Yes, tomorrow is my official day."

"Are you riding your bike or bus?"

Adam said, "Nah, my mom will be taking me to school and pick me up. She has to sign some papers and speak with the principal and meet the nurse, so I got it easy tomorrow."

"Neato," Bobby replied. "Hey, tomorrow, meet me at the cafeteria by the blue garbage can. I'll introduce you to the crew."

"Sure, that sounds great, Bobby," replied Adam.

"Okay, well, I better get back home. I have some homework to do. We have to write a paper for Ms. White's class."

"Who's Ms. White?"

"Oh, she's our beautiful English teacher, you'll see, she's gorgeous." Bobby smiled all big and cheesy.

Adam chuckled and said, "Okay, well, take care of my comic books, and I'll see you tomorrow." He gathered the comics and started walking down the stairs to the entryway.

He stopped and said very shy and soft, "Thank you for the cookies and milk, Mrs. Garcia, they were delicious. Nice to have met you, Mrs. G., I mean, Garcia."

Mrs. Garcia giggled and said, "You're welcome, Bobby, come back soon."

Bobby ran back home and then noticed that he forgot his mitt and ball on the grass, so he went back outside and picked them up in one hand and had Adam's comic books in the other hand, shut the door, and ran back to his room. Bobby couldn't wait to look at the comic books. Bobby's mom asked, "Did you meet the new kid on the block?"

Bobby said, "I sure did!" Bobby was speaking so fast and excited that Bob's mom asked him to slow down. "Yes, Mom, I met him, and he's really neat. His name is Adam. His mom is super nice and bakes stuff all the time. When I went over there, the house smelled like a bakery. She made some chocolate chip cookies and gave us some milk. Oh my, it was delicious," Bobby replied all excited. "And then Adam took me up to his room and showed me his trophies and comic books. He even let me borrow a couple, see!" Bobby held up the comic books to his mom.

She smiled and said, "That's good, Bobby, they sound like very nice people."

"They are." Bobby added, "I didn't meet his dad yet, but his mom is beaut—" Bobby stopped before he stuck his foot in his mouth, "I mean, she's a really nice lady, Mom!"

Bobby's mom smiled and said, "Okay, well, I think it's time to do some homework before supper. You have about an hour. Your father should be home soon."

"Okay, Mom, sure will!" Bobby reached into his carrying sack and pulled out his paper and English book. Ms. White had mentioned that they should read a few pages tonight, so Bobby sat at his desk that was made out of wood. His desk had a small lamp and an alarm clock and a few keepsakes on it. He loved military toys, so of course, Bobby had two tanks small in size (the size of the palm of your hand), some army soldiers, a few dinosaurs, a bag of marbles, and a pen and pencil holder sitting on top of his desk. Bobby opened the English book up and started to read. He read very slow as if he was sounding out each word. After about an hour, Bobby heard his dad's car and bookmarked his book with a piece of paper then ran outside to meet his dad.

He got to his dad's car, which was a light baby blue 1945 Mercury. Bobby ran outside and greeted his dad by opening his door. "Hey, Dad, how are you?"

Bobby gave him a hug, and his dad hugged him and scuffed the top of his head and replied, "Good, son, good! Hard day today, a bit tired."

"Can I help you with your briefcase?"

"Sure," his dad replied. "What did you do today, Bobby?"

"I went to school then came home and came outside to play some catch with my mitt, and I met the new kid. He's real neat, Dad!"

"Well, that's just great to hear, Bobby. What's his name?"

Bobby replied, "His name is Adam Garcia, and he let me borrow a few of his comic books."

"Oh yeah, Bobby, what kind of comic books?"

"Archie and Superman!"

"Sounds fun, Bobby. Where's your mother?"

Bobby replied, "In the house cooking dinner, it's just about ready."

"Good, I'm starved," Bobby's dad answered. Bobby's dad's name was Paul, but he was called Mr. Schutzer at work. He was a tall broad-shouldered man with a height of six feet four, light skinned, and with freckles and dark-red-brown hair. His voice was very deep. His hands were so large that he could grab Bobby's face in one hand. His feet were so large—size eighteen. Bobby would play walk-around in his shoes; they were like skis. Soon, Mrs. Schutzer called out, "Supper is ready, wash up, Bobby, and come to the supper table." They all met and bowed their heads for grace. "Amen," Bobby exclaimed. "Thank you, Mom and Dad, for this delicious food. I'm starved."

"Me too, Bobby," Bobby's dad replied. His mom and dad spoke of their day at work while he ate. He couldn't wait to finish his supper to rush back to his room and read a comic book before going to sleep. So after Bobby finished, his mom and dad were still eating. Bobby asked to be excused. They both said, "Yes, son, go ahead and take your plate to the sink and rinse, and then you may go to your room."

"Thank you, Mom, the pot roast was so yummy. My favorite!" Bobby sat his plate in the sink and rinsed then wiped his hands and walked past the supper table back to his room. Bobby picked up one of the comic books: *Superman and the Red Villain*. He opened it slowly as if Superman was going to fly out. Bobby was so excited to read the comic book. Each page was crisp clean. He slowly read the comics out loud. He made sure to take easy care of the pages, making sure not to rip them. Bobby loved the pictures. He rushed over to his desk to grab a piece of paper and sketched a pie of the *S* on superman's chest then slowly drew a picture of Superman and the villain. It was a pretty decent drawing, and next to the pictures, Bobby wrote down the names "Superman and villain," but on the spelling, he switched up the letter *a* with an *i*; and on *Superman*, he spelled *super* backward, and wrote *nam* instead of *man*. As Bobby was reading the comic book, he drifted off to sleep with the comic book and drawing on his chest and next to him. His parents came in to talk to him and noticed him asleep. Before they woke him to get into his pajamas and into the covers, they noticed his spellings on his drawings, and both looked at each other with sadness. Mr. Schutzer said, "Hey, Bob, it's bedtime, go ahead and get your pajamas on and go to sleep. We'll talk to you tomorrow."

"We love you, son," Bobby's mom added.

"Love you too, Mom and Dad." His parents left his room and went back to the kitchen and talked about Bobby's problem. They discussed spending more time with him, researching, and to speak to all of his teachers starting with Ms. White tomorrow.

Nothing really exciting at the other kids' houses, except that one of Jason's dad's employees cut his hand today on one of the butcher knives, so his papa came home early. He had to shut down the deli early today, so he played ball (catch) with Jason after school.

Over at Jody's house, she helped her grandma fix supper and decided to do her homework early. That way, she can just sit up after supper and watch TV with her grandma. Jody's parents died in a car accident when she was just three years old. Her grandparents raised her since then, but her grandfather passed away from a heart attack two years ago, so Jody helped out a lot with chores and cooking whenever she got the chance. They had a very close bond with each other. Jody would do anything for her grandma, who she called Momo. Jody's Momo usually would brush her hair and braid it at least once or twice a week. It wasn't uncommon to find them sitting at the small supper table putting puzzles together or playing cards. Her Momo would have bridge night every Wednesday at her house. Usually, five of her friends would come over and play. She loved bridge night because all of her friends would bring sweet goodies. She would grab a few and sit in the living room and watch the television until her Momo would say in a sweet, loud voice, "Jody, honey, it's getting about that time for bed."

Jody would always reply with a sweet voice, "Okay, Momo." Jody's grandma always felt so sad for Jody for losing her parents at such a young age and not having a brother or sister to grow up with, so Jody's grandma would try to be as adventurous as possible. When Jody's grandpa was alive, they would take little road trips everywhere in his pickup truck and chrome streamline camper trailer, but since her grandpa passed away a few years ago, Jody's grandma didn't travel outside the little town, and she sold her grandpa's truck and trailer.

Jody's grandma has a beautiful Cadillac, black in color, big white walls, and shiny chrome curb finders. Jody would often say, "Can I drive your car, Momo, when I get old enough?"

Her grandma would always say, "Sure, Jody." Often when Grandma would drive to town, she'd always wear big hats, a scarf, and sunglasses. Jody would often wear a scarf and sunglasses too. It was adorable to see them driving around in town.

Grandma was also a member of the PTA, so when she went to town to pick up a few items from the grocery store, she'd stop by a friend or two's place and sit and mingle with a cup of tea or coffee before heading back to the house. For the most part, Jody was a very good girl. Very creative, smart, funny, and very lovable—her grandma would tell her friends in the PTA and when she would have bridge night at the house. She was very proud of Jody.

At Sarah's house, it was a little different story. Her dad was a salesman. He was a hardworking man who came home every night and expected the house to be clean and supper on the table hot for him. He often walked through the back door after parking the car in the garage, open the refrigerator, pull out a beer, and sit right down at the end of the supper table. Sarah and her sister would be in the kitchen helping Mom get supper ready. Sarah and her younger sister Rebecca would stop what they were doing and hug their papa hello. He'd hug them and would say in Spanish, "Go ahead and finish helping your mother." He'd then ask where the boys were. Sarah's mother would answer, "In their room." Sarah had one older brother who was a freshman in high school and one younger brother who was in between Sarah's and her sister's ages. Their names were Lucas, age fifteen, and Gilbert, age ten. Sarah's parents would talk to each other in Spanish but talk to the kids in English. Sarah and Lucas knew a little Spanish, but the littlest ones didn't know very much Spanish to converse with Spanish-speaking people. So Sarah was bilingual but would hardly use it unless they were around other family members or friends who spoke the language. It was typical that the boys never helped with supper; only if Sarah's dad barbequed outside, then the boys were expected to watch and help. Sarah and the kids and the mother seemed to be timid when their dad was home. Often, you would hear Sarah's mother and father yelling at night in their bedroom. The kids would put the pillows over their heads to drown out the yelling. Each morning, her mom would have breakfast made: eggs, beans, and tortilla. Sometimes, she would make potatoes. Her father would leave at 7:00 a.m. to start the day bright and early. He would never speak in the morning. He would be dressed in a white shirt and tie with black freshly polished shoes. His jacket would still be hanging in the bedroom, and his fedora would be hanging on the hat rack in the entryway. During his breakfast, he would read the paper. When the clock struck seven, Sarah's mom would go to the bedroom and grab her dad's coat and slip it on him and then go grab his hat off the rack and hand it to him.

He always leaned in for her to kiss him on the cheek, then he would say, "Have a good day in school, kids. No getting into trouble, you all hear?"

They all would answer quickly, but Gilbert wouldn't sometimes, and Papa's voice would get louder and stronger, and Gilbert would say, "Yes, Papa!"

"Good! Make me proud, kids!"

After Sarah's dad would leave, they all would give a sigh of relief. Her mom was so much easier and calmer and more talkative than their dad.

CHAPTER 6

Monday night came and gone, and they all did their homework and went to sleep. Next morning (Tuesday), they rose and walked to the bus stop where the bus picked them all up at different times. So when they all got on the bus, they all went to the back. When Bobby got onto the bus, he had a huge smile and said, "Helllllloooooo, everybody. Guess what?"

They all answered, "What's up, Bobby?"

"I met the new kid, and he's super neat!"

"What?" Jody and Sarah said, "Really?" as their voices got all excited and high-pitched.

Jason said, "I thought you didn't like him."

"Yeah, well, I was wrong. We played basketball yesterday for a bit, then he showed me his room and his comic book collection. His mom is so pretty!" Bobby caught himself then said, "I mean, she's so nice, she baked us some cookies, they were so delicious."

Sarah asked, "What kind of cookies?"

Bobby answered, "Chocolate chip walnut. Mmmmm, I can still taste them."

Jason added, "So you said he had a comic book collection?"

"Yeah, he takes great care of them. They all have plastic covers on them, he even let me borrow a few to read. I brought them with me to read between times of class or at break or lunch, whenever. He said he'd be coming to school today. I told him to meet us at the blue garbage can. What do you think, guys?"

The girls said, "Oh yes, we can't wait to meet him."

Jason seemed a little put off but said, "Go, sure, let's meet this jokester." The girls seemed to play with their hair and acted all giggly. The bus pulled up to the front of the school, and they all filed off the bus and walked to Ms. White's class. Jason pulled out a shiny apple and sat it on her desk and smiled all smoothly at Ms. White as she smiled and said, "Well, thank you, Mr. Ferrahi, that's very kind of you to bring that for me. I'll have to enjoy that in my lunch." She winked at him. Jason stumbled into the desks and laughed it off and cleared his throat.

"Good morning, Bobby."

Bobby's face went from a smile to a half smile. "Hello, Ms. White, how are you?"

"I'm good, Bobby." She then asked the class to open their books to page 110 and start reading and that she would be back. "Follow me, Bobby, I need some help with some papers." Bobby smiled and left with Ms. White to go to the principal's office to sit in an empty office and take a brief test. "But before you do this, Bobby, your parents are here to speak to me, so sit still, and I will be back. You can sort these papers for me until I come back." Ms. White left Bobby and went into the vice principal's office and had a little meeting with Bobby's parents. She shook their hands softly and sat down.

She explained what Bobby was having problems with. "I didn't catch it right off the bat, but I've noticed a few things that Bobby does when he writes. I'm hoping to help him through it. I've notified all the teachers, and we are all on the same team. We want Bobby to succeed and grow to work through this difficult situation."

"We agree," Mr. and Mrs. Schutzer answered. Ms. White then explained that she was going to give him a little test with multiple questions, a few pictures to coordinate with words, and write a few sentences—stuff like that. Bobby's parents agreed then shook her hand and then left. Ms. White gathered the test together and walked back to the room where Bobby was sitting.

"Thank you, Bobby, for sorting these papers. What a great job!" She patted him on his shoulder. Then she said, "Here are three pages. Just do the best that you can. If you don't understand, leave it blank. Here is a scratch paper to write stuff out to figure it out. I'll give you the whole class to do this, Bobby. I'll come and get you if you're not done by the time class is done."

"Okay, Ms. White," Bobby said with a smile.

"Okay, I'll see you soon." She shut the door behind her. Bobby sat at the first question for a few minutes then continued through each question. He seemed to answer most of them easily, but some of it really stumped him. The multiple questions seemed to be easy for him. Approximately fifteen minutes later, he turned to page 2 and started to go through those questions with some difficulty. After about twenty minutes, he turned to page 2 over then went on to page 3. After about twenty-five minutes, Ms. White came in and asked him how he was doing. Bobby answered, "I just have three more questions."

"Okay, I need to make a few copies, and I will be right back."

Bobby continued to do his test. Soon, he finished up and put his pencil down. He held his head up like it weighed a hundred pounds. Ms. White came in and asked if he was okay; he said, "Yeah, I guess."

She said, "Okay, Bobby, I'll get back to you probably in a week or so. Don't worry too much about this. We just want to help you more, that's all. So here is a hall pass to go to your next class, make sure you go to the restroom if you need to and get a drink of water."

"Oh, Ms. White, is there any homework for tonight?"

"Just to continue to read and study for the test on Friday."

"Okay, thank you, see you tomorrow," Bobby said with a worried face. Bobby took a big sigh while he dragged his feet while walking. When he got to the hall outside of the principal's office, he ran into

Jody. Jody greeted him with a big smile. Her braids were perfect with bows in them.

"How you doing, Bobby?"

"Oh, I guess I'm okay."

"Did you take that test for Ms. White?"

"Yeah, it was a little hard, but I answered almost every question."

"That's good, Bobby. I'm sure you did okay. Like I said, if you ever need any help, I'm always here. We're friends, right?"

"Yeah, okay then."

"Bobby, ask me if you need help." At that moment, Bobby felt something for Jody. Her eyes were so blue and shiny—sparkly like diamonds—and her hair was of golden color. Bobby's face felt hot all of a sudden. He felt shy and embarrassed a little for feeling this way for Jody. He had never felt this way before with anybody. Jody was talking about other stuff, but he didn't hear a word she said, even though he was looking right at her. Jody spoke loudly, "Do you hear me, Bobby?"

He mumbled back, "Uh, yea, so we'll meet at lunch then. Adam is supposed to meet us all."

"Okay, Bobby, cheer up, it's gonna be okay."

"Okay, Jody." Bobby waved to Jody, standing still as if he was paralyzed. She waved back to him with a big ole smile. Bobby's heart was pounding so hard in his chest. Two more classes went by, and then the bell rang for lunchtime. They met at the hallways and walked over to the cafeteria, where they all stood around waiting for Adam. Soon after, Bobby noticed Adam in the distance walking toward them. Bobby waved, and Adam waved back. Jody and Sarah asked each other if their hair looked okay. They both started messing with their hair, looking into a little mirror. Sarah said, "Do you have ChapStick?"

Jody answered, "Oh yes, I do." So while they were fussing over their selves, Adam walked up. He was wearing jeans, rolled up, showing his bright-white socks with his penny loafers. He had a black buttoned-up shirt with a lightweight zip-up jacket. He's all, "Hey, Bobby! How you doing?"

"I'm good, Adam, I'd like you to meet the crew." Bobby put his hand on Jason's shoulder and introduced him. "This is my best friend, Jason Ferrahi, he's the one whose dad has the deli downtown."

"Nice!" Adam added. "My name is Adam Garcia. Nice to meet you, Jason." They shook hands.

"These are my other good friends Jody Jenkins and Sarah Fruentz."

"Wow," he mumbled under his breath. "Nice to meet you both. How were your morning classes?"

"Good," they answered all flirty and shy.

Giggling after, he said, "Maybe you gals could show me around."

They briefly showed him, but it's going to take him a while to remember. "My first class is Ms. White, English, I think."

They all answered all at once, "Our favorite teacher. She's so fun and sweet."

Bobby and Jason said, "Oh, man, she's so pretty!"

Jody and Sarah said, "Shut up, guys!" They all laughed after.

"What's for lunch?" Adam asked.

Bobby answered quickly because if there is one thing that Bobby knows, it is the lunch menu. "They're serving pizza, french fries, salad, and I think spaghetti."

"Oh, that sounds great. I'm so hungry. Let's go!" It seemed everybody liked Adam. After they got their plates, they sat all together on a table inside.

"Sarah and Jody always have their lunch packed," Jason added.

"That's super neat," Adam added. Adam asked Bobby how he liked the comic books.

Bobby said, "Oh my gosh, Adam, I love them. I only got halfway through *Superman*."

"Oh, okay, that's all right, hang on to them until this weekend. I'll show you more then."

Bobby said, "Okay, that's super nice of you."

Jason asked, "So do you like playing sports?"

Adam answered, "Yes, I love basketball and swimming, do you guys have a swimming pool here?"

"Yeah, we do," Jason said sternly.

Then Jody asked Adam, "Where did you come from?"

"Well, we just moved here last week. We used to live about eight hundred miles away in Herringbone, Colorado. Nice place, but my dad's work was transferred here."

"What kind of work does your dad do?"

"He's in the military."

"Oh, really?"

"Yeah," Adam answered. "He's in the Air Force."

Bobby asked, "Is he a pilot?"

"Yeah, he is, Bobby."

"Cool! That explains all the model airplanes you have hanging in your bedroom."

"Yeah, I get a few models for my birthday or Christmas. When my dad has time off, he'll help me a little building them."

"*Wow*, that sounds fun," Jason added. "I'd like to see them sometime."

"Sure," Adam answered, "you guys should all come over this weekend. We'll play some basketball and hang out. I'll see if my mom will make us sandwiches and cookies."

"That sounds so nice, Adam," Sarah added while she flipped her hair and batted her eyes.

Adam smiled and said, "All right, sounds good." Adam then asked each of them about their parents. Bobby told him that his parents were teachers at the college a town away.

Jason mentioned that his dad owned a deli, and his mom stayed home and cooked and cleaned and did the shopping. Just about the time for the girls to tell him about them, the lunch bell rang. Lunch was over.

"Okay, gals, do you think you could show me where I'm supposed to go?"

They said, "Sure, *Adam*!" Bobby noticed how the girls were acting and actually mentioned how it bothered him a little.

Jason said to Bobby, "Hey, what, do you have a crush on the girls?"

He said, "No," all loud and stern!

"Ooooh, Bobby, yes, you doll!" Jason was laughing. "Oh, buddy, you have a crush on them!"

Bobby answered strongly, "*No*, I don't! I just like Jody!" "What! You like Jody? When did this happen, champ! Oh my gosh, Bobby! You really like Jody?"

Bobby answered, "Yeah, I think. She is always so sweet and friendly with me, and after me taking that stupid test of Ms. White, she was walking by when I came out of the principal's office, and she patted me on the shoulder and was all smiley, and at that moment, my heart started racing. My face got hot too."

Jason covered his mouth as if he was going to cough but laughed through his fist. "Wow! Bobby, I can't believe that."

Bobby then added, "Yeah, she would never go for a guy like me. Look at me, I have red curly hair and blue eyes. I'm not skinny like you or the girls or Adam."

"Well, you're not fat, buddy. Don't beat yourself up. Just be friends and see if anything happens. We have a lot of time to figure out things. That's pretty cool though, Bobby. You the man." Jason added, "Anyway, I like Adam, he's super friendly. We can play sports with him. Should we tell him about Wednesday's meeting with the golden box?"

"Nah, we'll tell him this weekend."

"Okay, sounds good."

"Okay, well, I gotta go to my class. I'll see you in PE. See ya later, buddy!" They waved and went their ways. The day went on, then the bell rang at two forty-five.

"Yeah! School's out," Jason yelled. They all met at the bus except Adam.

The girls asked, "Is Adam riding the bus today?"

Bobby answered, "*No*, his mom is picking him up." Shortly after, they all noticed a turquoise convertible Thunderbird pull up with a beautiful woman driving it. Jason grabbed Bobby's chest and back as if he was hugging him and said, "Oh my gosh, is that Adam's mom? *Wow!*" Jason carried on. "She's hot!"

Bobby answered in a dazed moan, "Yeaaaa, she is. She is super pretty." Even the girls mentioned that she was beautiful like a model, like Marilyn Monroe. They stood in a stare, watching Adam walk to the car. Adam got in the passenger side, put his cool shades on, and waved to us staring by the bus. We waved back. His mom even waved.

"Did you see that?" Sarah said.

CHAPTER 7

So they all went on the bus except Adam, then each was dropped off at their bus stop, except Bobby got off at Jason's stop just to hang out a little before going home. They all talked about Wednesday being the day to meet and bring their treasures they found. All of them displayed their findings in their room after they cleaned and shined their pieces. When Bobby got off at Jason's stop, they both walked slowly, picking up rocks and tossing them. They talked about Adam and girls and laughed and joked a lot. Before they headed to Jason's house, they walked down Wilks Avenue, where the creepy house was. They had a few blocks to go before they got there, so they took their time. Bobby told him that he asked his mom about the place of the house, and she said that the place was abandoned. Bobby thought that was wrong because both Jason and Bobby saw the ladies and all the cats. So this time, Bobby and Jason decided to see again for themselves, so they tossed little rocks in front of them as a game to see who could get closer to the fence or closer to a stick or brick. So Jason decided to toss it farther, and when he did, it bounced off a tire that was sitting on the side of the street and bounced up and hit one of the cats that was sitting near the fence of the creepy house, and the cat shrilled a meow and took off running, which made other cats follow. So Bobby and Jason ran up to where Jason hit the cat to check and see if the cat was okay, but the cats were all gone. No cats. It appeared that nobody was home, so they slowly creaked open the wooden gate that had bushes and ivy overgrown on it. It barely opened with all the overgrowth. Bobby and Jason pried open the gate, just enough to squeeze through the gate. They both stayed close with each other and low. They both looked around and, behind them, saw that nobody was there or around. They stepped slowly up the steps that led to the wooden porch. There were dry rotten boards, leaves everywhere, cobwebs hanging from the upstairs awning, and wooden pillars.

There was an old wooden swing that was still hanging. They slowly stepped to the windows to see if they could get a clear look inside the house, but most of the windows were covered too much. They did, however, find a very small space to view the inside, and it looked as if nobody has been there for years and years.

"Weird," Bobby said out loud.

"I know," Jason added. "We saw those cats and women here! I mean, Bobby, where are all the cats? There must have been at least twenty of them."

"I dunno, Jason. It's crazy!" So they continued around the backside. The grass was dead and overgrown as the trees and bushes were in the front. They went up to the back door and slowly turned the knob.

"Oh!" Bobby said with a surprised voice. "Oh my gosh, the doors are unlocked, wanna go in, Jason?"

"Okay, sure. Wait, let me get a stick. Yeah, okay." So Jason got a stick then ran back up where Bobby was. They slowly opened the door where it creaked, like the door hadn't been oiled in a hundred years. They walked in, in sync, small footsteps together as they looked around, and listened to every noise. They went from the back of the service porch area where a washing machine and a sink would be then walked through the kitchen. They continued through a swinging door that closed off the kitchen to the dining room. Bobby swung the door open and said, "Cool, look at this table. It was an oak-looking dining table where the legs of it looked like hand-carved gargoyles. The eyes had small ruby jewels attached. Jason said, "Wow. That's unreal."

Bobby then pointed to the chandelier above the dining table. "Look, it has ruby and black-colored jewels in it."

Jason said, almost in a whispering voice, "Hey, doesn't it kind of look like Sarah's necklace that she found in the dump?"

"Nooooo," Bobby answered with a little giggle. "Let's go check out upstairs and see what's up there. It's obvious that nobody has been here for years. I wonder who used to live here." They walked through the house slowly. They started up the wooden staircase, every step creaked, there was no sneaking around this house, you could hear a fly land on the wooden steps. They got up to the landing and looked down and said, "Wow, that looks like far away to fall from." So they then went into one room, opened the walk-in closet, and all of a sudden, a cat meowed, shrilling out and hissing. It scared Bobby and Jason so bad that they fell back onto their backs. "Omg! See, there were cats here." They hopped up, and as they did, they heard something wrestle in another room, followed by what sounded like footsteps.

Jason and Bobby ran so fast that they almost flew down the stairs. Bobby kept saying, "Oh my gosh, oh my gosh, hurry, Jason, hurry." They flew down the stairs and down through the family room then heard the creaks on the floor as if the steps of someone were getting closer. Jason grabbed the front doorknob, but it had been deadlocked or nailed shut. Bobby yelled, "Through the back, Jason, c'mon!" They slid around on the hardwood floors almost standing still. Sliding around, they scuffled over each other to get outside. They both fell to the ground running down the steps at the back. They crawled and shuffled to get their footing and ran toward the front. All of a sudden, there were at least twenty cats; they all circled the two boys like they hadn't eaten in weeks. Jason and Bobby yelled out, "Move, cats. Move!" They were so close to the gate when a woman appeared—an older woman with a long dark dress on, dark hair, and dark eyes. She was pointing and mumbling words. Then out of nowhere, there were two others that looked almost identical to the first one. They stood in a triangle with their hands raised above their heads; then in a circular motion, and words they didn't understand, threw an imaginary force around Bobby and Jason. They froze. Fright in their eyes, they couldn't speak or move. One of the ladies said, "Beware, you don't belong here. You'll be cursed, for you have the times that dwell, the cards have turned, for you will follow as long as you continue." At that point, the wind picked up, and leaves started blowing in a circular motion. Tears rolled down both of their cheeks, still frozen still. They both then dropped to their knees and started crawling out the rest of the way from the front yard and through the old wooden gate. They then split up and ran separate ways all the way home. They didn't look back, they didn't slow down, they just ran as fast as they could. When Bobby got home, he ran right past his mom into the house and into his room and put his head on the bed and covered it with a pillow. His mom was getting a few bags from the car in the front driveway.

When Jason got home, he ran right into his room and laid down on his bed and put the pillow over his head. They both were out of breath. Both of their moms followed them into their rooms and asked what was wrong.

"Why were you running so fast?" They both tried to explain that they went into the yard of the abandoned house because Bobby accidentally threw his ball over the fence.

Bobby said that Jason threw his ball over the fence, that's why they were in the abandoned house's yard. Both lying a bit but out of breath trying to explain what they saw. Their mothers both told them to slow down a bit and say what happened. At about that point, they both decided to not say anything else until they get their story straight. So they would have to talk about it tomorrow unless Bobby could break away and go see Jason. It still was pretty early to take a bike ride over to Jason's, so Bobby shrugged off his terrified look and breath and asked his mom if he could ride over to Jason's, that he forgot a piece of paper of his for homework from Ms. White.

She said, "Yes, but after you help me put the groceries away."

"Okay, Mom," Bobby answered. Soon after he finished, he grabbed his bicycle out of the garage and hopped on it and started pedaling over to his place. He made sure not to ride by the house on Wilks and Fifth and pedaled fast over to Jason's. He then arrived at Jason's and knocked on the door. Jason's mom answered.

Bobby then asked Mrs. Ferrahi, "Is Jason here, ma'am?"

She said, "Go ahead, he's in his room." He walked into his room and shut the door.

"Hey, Jason, did we see what we saw?" Jason replied as if he was in shock.

"Yeah, Bobby, we did."

Bobby then asked, "Were there no cats around, and we went inside, and nobody was around, and then all of a sudden, there was a cat and those creepy-looking ladies, then lots of cats and wind. Did you feel paralyzed? Could you move? Because I couldn't!"

Jason grabbed Bobby and shook him and yelled under his breath, "Bobby, you got to get ahold of yourself. I don't know if we should tell anyone about this. I tried to tell my mom and couldn't get it all out."

"*Me* too, Jason," Bobby whispered in a yelling kind of way.

"Well, what do we do?"

"Nothing, *we* do nothing! We don't go over there anymore, we don't talk about it, we just forget it."

But Bobby started to mumble. "*No!*" Jason looked Bobby in the eyes. "*No!* We're not gonna talk about it unless we agree together. Okay!"

"Okay," Bobby said.

They both sat on the bed in shock, holding their heads; then all of a sudden, they started laughing.

"Oh my gosh, that was so crazy, Jason, I can't believe we did and went through that. Are you okay?"

"Yeah, I just skinned my knee, how about you?"

"I have a cut on my arm and bruised my leg and knee. Man, what a crazy experience, huh!"

"Yeah." They both laughed quietly, making sure Jason's mom didn't hear them clearly.

"Okay, so we won't say anything quite yet to our parents then.What about the gang? The girls?"

"Maybe," Jason said.

So Bobby said, "Okay, I'll see you at school tomorrow. Take the bus, then we'll take it back home then meet up at the school baseball field." So Bobby pedaled back home, parked his bicycle in the garage, went into the house, and asked his mom if there was anything he could help with.

She replied, "Yes, Bobby, can you please take out the garbage and gather your dirty clothes and take the sheets off your bed and the towels in the bathroom and take them to the washroom. I'll start the laundry shortly." She first seasoned some chicken and vegetables for supper then slipped them into the oven to cook. So Bobby walked back to his room and gathered the dirty clothes then took the garbage out to the sanitation can in the alley then walked back into the house and went to his room and started reading the comic book that he borrowed from Adam. He opened the *Archie* comic book. It was funny instead of serious, so he read and laughed, getting his mind off of what had happened to him and Jason. Bobby read the whole comic book then slipped the plastic cover over it and sat it neatly on top of his desk then opened up his English book to page 110 then started reading and making a few study notes since he didn't get a chance to read during class.

Jason opened up a *Spider-Man* comic book and read through it slowly. He had already read it two times already, but each time seemed to be the first. After about halfway through, Jason fell asleep for a bit. He then started to dream about the weather changing, windy and rainy. He then woke all panicked and figured out that it was just a dream. He then went into his kitchen where his mom was cooking some pasta and asked if there was anything to snack on.

His mom replied, "Yes, dear, I baked a chocolate cake today. Would you like a small piece, son, and some milk?"

"Yes, Mom, I had a hard day today. I feel so tired."

His mom got him a small slice of cake and milk then felt Jason's forehead. "Well, son, you don't feel like you're getting a cold. Perhaps you just didn't get a good night's sleep last night, or you played too hard at your sports. You let me know if you feel worse soon. Your dad probably won't be home until after suppertime since Vinny cut his hand yesterday. Your father has a shipment coming in late, so he'll be home late. It's just you and me for supper, son."

"Okay, Mama, sounds nice."

She did ask for a favor. "After you're done, son, can you take the garbage out and grab the sheets off the laundry clothesline and bring them in?"

"Yes, Ma, no problem."

After Jason finished his cake, he took the garbage out and pulled the sheets off the line. He then noticed some thundering and dark clouds in the distance. He didn't know that there was going to be rain, so he went inside and asked his mom if it was supposed to rain.

She answered, "No, honey, I don't think so."

He then mentioned to his mom that he saw thunder and dark clouds. She then said, "That's very strange. We're not supposed to have any rain for a few weeks. Well, thank you for telling me. I'll watch to make sure it doesn't when I put clothes out to dry. I'll have to use the dryer." They were the few in the town that had a dryer. You had to have money to have a dryer at that time. Jason went back to his room and studied some English. He then waited for supper to be ready and to be called by his mom. The evening continued, and Jason went to sleep early this night. Jason was woken up around midnight when the tree outside his window kept scratching at his window from the wind. It looked like it was going to rain but never did; it just was super windy through the night. It made it very difficult to sleep.

CHAPTER 8

The night passed, and everybody woke bright and early, but Jason felt sluggish, not his usually peppy self. He took a shower, got ready, and ate breakfast as the rest of the crew did. At Bobby's house, Bobby woke very sluggishly as well. He almost asked his mom if he could stay home, but if he did that, then he couldn't meet everybody at the baseball field after school with the golden box. So he pushed through his sleepy mode. They all ate their breakfast then continued to their bus stop to wait for the bus pickup. Each and every one of them got on the bus; Bobby usually was the last to get on the bus. And when he did today, he walked very slow with a slight limp. He got to the back, and the girls noticed Jason and Bobby acting a little different.

They asked, "What's the matter with you two?"

"Nothing," the boys answered.

"Are you sure?"

"Yeah," Jason said, "I just feel a little under the weather."

Jody asked, "Bobby, are you okay? You have circles under your eyes."

"Yeah, I'm okay, just sleepy. Did you guys hear the wind last night?"

"What?" Sarah said.

"Yeah, the wind," Jason added.

"Uh, nooooo!" Jody said after.

"What? The wind blew so hard at my house that it was hard to sleep."

"Yeah, at my house too," Bobby added.

"No," the girls said. "There was no wind last night."

Bobby and Jason looked at each other with confusion. "Weird." As if they were in shock still.

"Hmmm," Jason scratched his head.

"*Oh* well," Bobby blurted out, "can I tell them? Cannn I, Jason?"

"You don't have time, just wait until lunchtime."

"Okay, Jason," Bobby answered, sighing heavily. Soon after, the bus came to the front of the school, and everybody filed off the bus and walked to their classes. As they walked to their class, Sarah and Jody were talking with each other, asking if they knew what they were going to tell them. They kept looking at Jason and Bobby to see if they'd spill some of the beans about the subject, but they didn't budge. Their first class with Ms. White was a blur like the rest until the lunch bell rang for lunch. They all met up. Jody asked Bobby if he had seen Adam today, and he replied no.

"Why, Jody?"

"Oh, I was just wondering, I haven't seen him."

"Nah, I think he had mentioned that, today, he had a doctor's appointment and that he wouldn't be back to school until Friday."

"Oh, okay, well, so what's the new news, boys?"

"Well, wait a minute, let's go get our food, Bob!" The boys left to go to the food line while the girls got a seat and waited.

Jason said to Bobby, "Do you think we should tell them?"

"Yeah, we should, at least to them."

"Okay, we'll tell them." So they got their food and headed back to the table where they were sitting and sat down.

Bobby blurted out, "Remember that creepy old abandoned house on Wilks and Fifth Street?"

"Yeah," they said.

"Well, Jason and I went by there yesterday, and something happened."

The girls dropped their sandwiches and, with a surprised look, said, "*What?* What happened?"

"Oh my gosh, girls, it was the scariest event that we've ever encountered."

"Really?" Sarah exclaimed.

Bobby said, "So Jason and I were walking home, and we decided to go by that house. Well, we went there once before, and there was an old lady and lots of cats hanging around, and the old lady whispered something when we went by. Well, yesterday, we went down Wilks Street and was tossing rocks to see who could win, and when Jason threw the rock, it hit a tire on the side of the road and bounced up and over and hit a cat. The cat screamed meow, and so we reached up to the cat, and when we got there, we didn't see any cats anywhere, so it made us walk in further to see where the cats all went. We didn't see any, so we continued to look around the back. We still didn't see any cats, so I turned the knob at the back door, and it was unlocked, so Jason and I went inside.

"We walked around slowly, and the dining table had red and black jewels, and the chandelier had red and black jewels like Sarah's necklace. In the bathroom, there was a silver brush like Jody's mirror, and then when we got to the upstairs bedroom, a cat came out of the closet and scared us so bad that we fell back then got up. And when we did, we heard someone walking, so Jason and I ran down and tried to go out the front door then slid on the hardwood flooring. Then we saw a ton of cats circling around.

We heard footsteps going down the steps, and we ran out the back door, fell down on the back grass or dirt, then all of a sudden, there were a ton of cats hanging around and an old lady in a dark dress. She looked so scary, she was whispering loudly some words about a time and stuff, and we froze, we couldn't move, it's like she was holding us, and tears fell from our face uncontrollably, then the wind picked up and leaves were whirling around.

"Then all of a sudden, Jason and I dropped to the ground, and we crawled all crazy fast to get out of there. She warned us about something. I don't know, girls, I never want to go around that house again. We both split up and ran to our homes, then later decided not to say anything to anybody except to you, girls. Isn't that wild?"

"Yessss!" the girls replied while holding their mouths.

"How scary, I think I would have peed myself," Jody said.

Jason said, "I almost did. I still don't know exactly what the lady said, but she held her hands up above her head and then pointed at us. It was like a prayer, but it felt dark and evil. So when we told you that the wind kept us up all night, and you said there wasn't any wind, it made us think that it was some of the wicked ladies' doings. Then we both woke up feeling weak and ill. I almost told my mom that I didn't want to go to school, but I'm feeling okay now."

"Yeah, me too," Bobby added.

"I can't believe all that, guys!" Jody expressed. "Wonder what that is all about."

Bobby rubbed his head and face, "I'm still baffled about it all."

Jason added, "So after school, we'll go home and grab the box and bikes." About that time, the lunch bell rang. They gathered their garbage and threw it all away then walked back to the classes and went their separate ways.

"See you guys after class." Everybody said bye and waved. The day went on, and the bell rang on the last class. It was 2:45 p.m., school was out. They all waited for the bus to open to get on. Shortly, the bus driver opened the door, and they all filed on. Each of them was dropped off at their stop, and they exited. They all had discussed to meet back at the baseball field at three thirty and to bring their items. Jason got off the bus and ran home, did a few things, then grabbed the box and started walking. Soon, Bobby came riding his bike to pick Jason. Jason hopped on, and they continued until they were at the baseball field. Soon, Jody and Sarah came. They all sat in a circle with the box in the middle. Jason pulled out the clock and sat next to the box, then Bobby pulled his pocket watch out and laid it next to the clock as Sarah took off the necklace and laid next to Bobby's watch, and Jody grabbed the mirror and looked into its crack then set it down next to everybody's items. Jason opened the drawer and pulled out the card and dice that were there. He asked everybody, "Wonder why there is an ace card and dice in here. Maybe the whole deck fit in there and another dice but got lost at the dump." *Yeah, maybe*, Jason thought. *Weird*. About that time, Jason and Bobby felt a little dizzy. They both grabbed their heads.

The girls asked, "What's wrong, guys?"

They both said in a low, lethargic voice, "We don't know." So Jason threw the card and dice up and over as they both felt like leaning back.

The girls, looking strangely at them, said, "You guys okay?" And about that time, the wind picked up, and leaves were blowing as if they were caught in a whirlwind funnel. It seemed so loud like cats were crying, then smoke appeared. They all grabbed each other's hands as if they were bracing themselves for something. Then all of a sudden, white smoke appeared, and poof! They instantly disappeared. A young kid was walking by about the time that this all took place. He looked around as though he had seen a ghost. He watched it all happen but felt confused, questioning himself if what he saw was exactly what he saw. Standing still, he looked around and around but didn't see them anywhere. He slowly walked on, questioning himself.

CHAPTER 9

The kids appeared in a barn. They were disoriented and still holding each other's hands. They let go of their hand and rubbed their eyes and faces. Jason asked, "Did that just really happen?"

Jody asked, "Where are we? Weren't we at the baseball field a second ago?"

All Sarah could say was, "Oh my gosh, oh my gosh, where are we?"

Bobby felt his body to check if he could feel himself. "What the heck is going on?" Jason stood up, and when he did, he noticed that he was wearing different clothes. He was wearing overhaul-type brown pants and a dirty-white shirt and a cowboy hat. The girls stood up, and they were wearing long skirts with boots. Their hair was braided in one big braid and tied with a piece of ribbon.

"*Oh my gosh,*" Bobby yelled. "What the heck!" He looked at his clothes, and he was wearing something very similar to Jason's and a cowboy hat as well. They all kept circling around while standing, looking at the building they were in. It looked like a barn with no animals. Jason walked over to an opening, which was the barn door, and peeked out.

"Oh my gosh, you guys, we're somewhere entirely different. How could this be? What happened, and how did we get here."

"We are going to get into soooo much trouble," Sarah added. Sarah and Jody started to cry with worry.

Bobby went and hugged them and said, "It'll be okay," but in Bobby's mind, he wanted to start crying as well. He was just trying to be strong for the girls.

Jason said in a stern voice, "I think we should stick together and go walk around and see what's going on." Jason went back over to where they were standing and picked up the clock. "It was this clock that did it."

"How? How could it be?" Bobby asked!

"I don't know!" Jason yelled. He opened the drawer to see if that would take them back to the baseball field, but it didn't do anything. Inside the drawer was the dice but no card. "I wonder if that has something to do with it all, you guys. Let's put our heads together and think." Jason started thinking about everything they said and did. Let's walk a little. When they walked out of the barn, they noticed that everybody in the distance looked like they were wearing the same type of clothes, Western wear, and with horses. In the near distance, they noticed buildings, but the buildings didn't look like where they lived. They were in the country somewhere. They slowly walked down and over, looking around like they were strangers, but everybody that walked past them took their hat off slightly and said, "*Good* day!" The kids soon came across another kid and kind of followed him.

The kid turned around and said, "What seems to be the problem?"

"Oh, nothing," Bobby answered. "We just wanted to ask you a question."

"Oh," the kid replied. "Well, what would you like to know?"

Jason asked, "Where are we?"

The kid looked confused and asked, "What do you mean 'where are you?' We're in town!"

"No," Jody asked, "what town is this?"

The kid laughed and asked, "Have you guys lost your minds? I sit right next to y'all in class."

Their jaws dropped and said, "What do you mean?"

The kid replied, "I don't know what kind of a joke your pulling, but I'm starting to get a little miffed about it. I don't have time for jokes and games. If you want to settle this the man's way, then put them up." The kid put up his dukes and started walking around as to egg the boys on to dare to strike him.

Jason and Bobby said, "No, we just want to know what town this is. We're not from here," they begged for him to understand.

The kid answered all angry, "We are in Kalamazoo, Michigan, now leave me alone." The kid shifted his shirt and vest and carried on in the opposite direction. The kids continued on and came upon swinging doors, and above the doors were a sign that said Saloon.

"What the heck," Jody sighed. They peeked in, and it was a bar. A few men were in there sitting at the bar. They had cowboy hats and boots on, and every man seemed to be carrying a gun. Jody and Sarah were so terrified. Jason seemed to be strong and the leader. Bobby seemed scared as well, just following Jason's lead. About that time, a loud man's voice said, "*Hey!* What are you kids doing looking in the saloon?"

"Oh, nothing," Jody said.

He then said, "Where are your parents at?"

"I don't know," Sarah and Bobby said.

"Well, y'all should get going now."

"Okay, sir," they all mumbled and scurried off.

About that time, they all heard their names called by a different woman. They stood still as to wait to see what would happen. They all waited for them to come to them. Soon, four women walked over to them and said, "Where have you been, we need to get back home to fix some supper."

"Your pa needs you to do some deeds around the ranch," a lady had said to Bobby. The others said very similarly to each of them. They all decided to go with the woman at that moment. They whispered to each other to meet at the barn tomorrow so they could get the hell out of there. "Okay." They nodded and left with the women that appeared to be their moms or relatives. Life seemed so different from where they were.

Each family had their own horses and cattle and pigs and chickens. Chores consisted of cleaning the pens and stables, adding straw to the barn's floor, and feeding the animals. The weirdest thing there was that things were lit up with candles. Not everybody had electricity, so cutting wood to keep the house warm or to cook with was the way of living. It was country life where every man physically worked for their families to survive. Their form of transportation was horses or donkeys, and they pulled what they called a carriage or buggy, which was a trailer-looking cart that was pulled by a horse or horses.

CHAPTER 10

Jody went with a slender-looking woman who was fully clothed in a long dress and a bonnet over her head. She was a beautiful woman with dark blonde hair and blue eyes. When they walked home, they walked to a very simple-looking home, which only had three rooms. There was a dark cast-iron unit, which apparently was used to cook on and also keep the house warm. The lady asked Jody to help her with putting some food items away under what seemed to be the counter for the kitchen. The dinner table was like a picnic table. As Jody was putting away the items, she heard another girl's voice. The girl called out to her mama, "should I bring Ellie down?" she asked. Her mama answered with, "Sure!"

Soon, another young lady appeared with a baby in hand. Apparently, it was her sisters. She had long straight dark-brown hair with fair skin and brown eyes. She had a few freckles and perfectly straight teeth. Jody froze with confusion; partly excited, partly sad and scared. The young girl said, "Jody can you help me?"

Jody replied, "What?"

"Can you come help me with your baby sister?"

Her mama said, "Jody, go help your sister Sierra with baby Ellie."

"Oh, okay." Soon, Jody was holding baby Ellie who was so beautiful. Ellie had big beautiful blue eyes and soft skin with chubby cheeks. Jody's heart melted with love instantly. Jody asked the mom, "Can I play with Ellie for a little bit?"

The mom said, "Yes, Jody, that'd be fine." After a few hours, the husband came home. He was dirty, dusty, rough looking, not shaved, and with dark hair and a short beard wearing a hat and cowboy boots. He sat his rifle and gun holster with a pistol gun on a rack by the front door. Sierra ran to her dad and hugged him. He hugged her and the mom and then came right over and called Jody doll and hugged her and the baby. All she could do was stare. The mom mentioned to the dad that Jody was acting a little strange, perhaps he needed to spend a little time with her before supper.

He asked, "What's for supper, Mom?"

She answered, "Some chicken soup and bread."

"Sounds great," he ended. He walked over to Jody and sat right next to her. "How's it going, doll?" he asked. "Did you have a bad day today?"

Jody replied, "No, I just feel a little under the weather, I think. How was your day, sir?"

"Aw, you know my day, I worked hard, doing a cattle run and fixing the buggy."

"Sounds interesting," she expressed. Jody stared into his blue eyes with a sense of comfortableness. Tears rolled down her face. For the first time, she felt like she was home and loved. It smelled so great in the small home. Jody thought to herself, *Oh my gosh, this is what it feels like to have parents and two sisters, a real family.* She instantly felt loved and warm.

The dad noticed a tear had fallen from her eye and said, "C'mon, doll, sit on my lap," and he held Ellie and Jody at the same time. Even though he smelled of musky dirt and sweat, it didn't matter because it was the best feeling ever. He looked into her eyes and said, "I'm sorry you feel sad right now but know that your mother and I and Sierra love you very, very much." Jody didn't want that moment to end. Moments later, the mother called Pa and Jody to the table to eat. They sat down and said grace then started eating the chicken soup. It tasted so good and warm since Jody seemed to be starving hungry. It had seemed like she hadn't eaten in days. The night grew later, supper was over, and the parents asked the girls to go to bed. They hugged their parents and went to their bedding. It was a loft above the living room with one big bed. It wasn't super soft but comfortable enough to lie their heads down to sleep. The bedding smelled like wood shavings. The blankets were made of wool material, and the bottom sheet was a straight piece of cotton. Their two pillows were made of what seemed like rolled blankets and tied on the ends with ribbon, and then they had two other pillows that were sacked like a cotton bag filled with chicken feathers. It was pretty comfortable. Jody felt so tired that she laid right behind Sierra and put her hand on her waist and fell right to sleep. Jody slept the rest of the night.

CHAPTER 11

When Bobby went with what seemed like his mother, she sent him right to the stables to feed and water the horses. They had four of them: two male and two female horses. Bobby was so terrified. He had never been next to an animal so large. He stood on one side of the wooden fence and thought to himself, *Oh no, I'm not getting in there with those horses*. Soon, two of the horses walked over close to Bobby and nudged his arm to tell him to pet them. Bobby softly and hesitantly rubbed their nose. He looked into their eyes. They seemed so big but pretty sweet. Bobby rubbed their soft snout. The one blew out his nose and made a snore-like sound. It scared Bobby so bad that he stepped back, but the horse was just enjoying Bobby petting them. "Hey, I guess you guys are okay," Bobby talked out loud to them as if they could understand, so he walked down farther; the horses slowly followed behind. Then Bobby climbed over the wooden fence and got into the corral. Bobby walked with the buckets of oats to the thing they called a food bin and water trough. He dumped the oats into the bin, and all four horses stood behind him then walked right up. Bobby was frozen being sandwiched in the middle of them. He slowly slipped in front of them and away. He looked into the water trough to see if they had enough water, but it appeared to be low. The water trough seemed to be kind of dirty but clear. It had algae growing on the sides a little, but the water was very clear, so Bobby figured he'd have to go and fill the buckets up and walk them back to the trough.

But where is the water? he asked himself, so he crawled out of the horse corral and looked around and around to find the faucet. All he saw was something coming out of the ground and some green weeds and grass around the base, so he walked over to it and stood approximately three feet from the ground. It had a spout and a handle-like thingy on top. Bobby sat the bucket down and grabbed the handle and tried to move it. When he did, a little bit of water came out, so Bobby moved the handle higher up and faster, and more water came out. *Oh my gosh, how unreal is this*, he thought to himself, so Bobby filled the buckets and walked back to the water trough. He took about five trips, back and forth and filled the five gallon bucket full of water, which was twenty five gallons total of water. He then pulled some alfalfa from the bails and put some in the feed bin. He then petted the horses then climbed out of the corral then walked back to the house.

He got to the front door, and a man yelled out to him from behind. "Did you lay straw in the barn, boy?"

Bobby replied, "Are you talking to me?"

The man said, "Yes, I don't see no other boy around."

Bobby muffled, "No, sir, I didn't."

The man said, "Well, you better get back out there and do it!"

"Okay," Bobby replied.

After Bobby did that, he started back up to the house. He shuffled his feet to kick off any mud or horse poop that was on his boots before he entered the house. The man that spoke to him said, "Don't you know, boy, you remove your hat at the door?"

"Oh yeah," Bobby replied.

The man seemed rough and mean. He yelled at the woman who took Bobby home (his mom), "Where is my supper, woman?"

The woman replied, "Right here, dear."

"What are we eating for supper tonight?"

"Chili beans with chunks of beef, bread, and squash."

"It sure smells good, Mom," Bobby spoke out.

"Go wash your hands, Bobby," she requested.

"Okay." Bobby looked around all confused and started walking where he thought was the restroom. When he walked into the restroom, all that was in there was a cabinet with a pan in the middle, a white pitcher of water, and a wooden-type tub. They didn't have running water, so Bobby took the pitcher of water and poured a little over his hands and then rubbed his hands together then rubbed his face. A cloth was hanging over the tub, so he grabbed it and wiped his face and hands then walked back to the kitchen where a small table sat with the man eating his supper. Evidently, this man was his father. He didn't speak, and when he did, he spoke as if he was angry. The woman didn't say a word. The house was so quiet. Bobby was afraid to say anything, so he just ate quietly, and when he was done, he asked his "mom" if there was anything that she needed help with. She answered, "No, Bobby, it's okay, go ahead and go to bed." Bobby went into the room where the bed was and lay down with his clothes on. He didn't know what to do. Shortly, after he went to lay down, he heard the man yelling and what seemed like hitting the woman.

Bobby put his hands over his ears and covers. Bobby couldn't
believe what he was hearing. All he could think was tomorrow that he hoped they could figure out how to get back home. Tears rolled down Bobby's face, then shortly after, he fell asleep.

CHAPTER 12

The lady that grabbed Sarah's hand was apparently Sarah's older sister. Sarah walked over to a horse pulling an open wooden buggy and followed the lady into the buggy. The lady smiled and said, "Hang on, Betsy, here (the horse) is acting up a little today."

Sarah said, "Okay, ma'am."

The lady grabbed the leather straps that came off the horse's mouth called reigns and whipped them up and down like a wave, and the horse started walking forward. The lady was soft-spoken but seemed very friendly and beautiful. She had a long dress with a corset-type top. She wore a big hat; it had a ribbon hanging where she tied under her chin. She glanced over at Sarah and smiled. Sarah kindly smiled back and asked where they were going. She said, "Back home, which is a little over the hill," then she added, "you know, silly."

Sarah then asked, "Who's at the house there?"

The lady then said, "Just Uncle Ted."

"Where's everybody else?"

The lady said, "Who?"

Sarah said, "I don't know, is anybody else going to be there."

She replied, "No, hun, you know it's just the three of us, nobody else. Hasn't been in a long time."

Sarah felt so scared and lost. She sat next to the lady and wondered, *Was she my sister or aunt or mother.* The horse and carriage pulled over the hill, and there was a beautiful small house sitting there. No grass but rose bushes all around a wooden white-painted fence and a small red barn off of the house property. There were two huge trees that umbrellaed over the house; one in the front side yard and one in the back. We pulled up, and she got out and stepped down. A man greeted us and grabbed the reigns from her. I stood up and stepped out and stood behind the lady. The man said in a raspy voice, "How was your day today, Sarah?"

"Good," Sarah answered.

"That's a girl."

"Did you want to go with your uncle Ted to go brush and feed Betsy (the horse)?"

"Uh," Sarah hesitated.

"Sure, go ahead, Sarah," the lady told Sarah. "I have to do a few things inside. I'll see you in a little bit. Go have fun with your uncle. You love brushing Betsy."

Uncle Ted told Sarah, "Here, grab the reigns, I'll let you drive back around to the barn."

"Really?" Sarah's eyes lit up like a star with excitement.

Ted then jumped on the passenger side and said, "Okay, pop the reigns up and down and talk to her." Shortly after, she did that. Betsy the horse started moving. Ted then said, "Pull one of the leather straps a little to the left a little, and she'll steer over to the left." Sarah did it, and Betsy started walking more to the left and around the side of the house. Sarah was so excited that she started laughing. Ted then said to ease up on the straps. Betsy started to go straight heading to the barn.

He then said, "Okay, now pull back a little on both straps," and Betsy started to slow down. "Okay," Ted said, "okay, pull hard and hold it back." Betsy stopped.

"Good *girl, Betsy, good girl*," Sarah praised.

Ted patted Sarah on the shoulder and said, "You're just like your mama was. A fast learner."

Sarah felt sadness, thinking that she lost her mother, but then realized that he was talking to a different mom and time. They both got out of the carriage, and Ted released a pin from the harness that Betsy the horse was wearing that was hooked to the carriage then walked her toward the barn and corral. Ted released her after he took her harness and reigned out of her mouth. He told Sarah to go over to the end of the barn and grab the two buckets. Sarah walked slowly over to where the buckets were, grabbed them, and brought them to Ted then said, "Follow me, Sarah." Ted walked over to a wooden bin that had some horse food in it. It looked like oatmeal. Ted said, "There are oats for Betsy, I just got a few sacks today of it. Hope she likes it." Sarah reached in and grabbed the metal scoop and scooped up a big amount and put it in the bucket. Uncle Ted said, "Go ahead and put another scoop in there." They then walked back over to where Betsy was and hung the bucket in front of her on the wooden fence where she would sleep. Ted said, "Follow me, we'll go pump some water in the bucket to add to her water trough. So they walked out of the barn and around to the water pump.

Sarah asked, "What's that, Uncle Ted?"

He looked at Sarah strangely and said, "You know, young lady, it's the water."

She covered her mouth with surprise and said, "Oh yeah." Sarah played it off well. So Sarah held the bucket as Uncle Ted pumped water into the bucket. They then walked back over to the barn and poured into Betsy's tub-like container called a trough. Ted told Sarah to grab Betsy's brush over there by the feed and bring it back to brush her. Ted said, "I have to do a few things around here, so go ahead and brush her tail but don't stand behind her where her legs are. She'll kick you."

"Okay, Uncle Ted."

Ted told Sarah, "Just brush her side and her hair on top called her mane." She's so beautiful, red-rust color with blonde-white hair and tail. Sarah spoke to Betsy, telling her that she's so pretty and soft. Sarah gave kisses to Betsy and looked into her big black-brown eyes and said softly, "I wonder what happened to my parents here. I wish I knew, big girl."

Shortly, after a bit, Ted came back and said, "Okay, Sarah, that's good enough. You did a great job. She sure loves you."

Sarah replied to Ted and said, "I love her too." Sarah kissed Betsy one last time on her soft nose and then told Ted she was going to go into the house to see if there's anything that she could help with.

Ted said softly, "Oh, that's very sweet of you, young lady. Your aunt Susie would love that."

She smiled then gave uncle Ted a big hug. He hugged her back He hugged her back and said, "Thank you for all your help."

"Tell your auntie I'll be in for supper in an hour or so."

"Okay," Sarah ran out of the barn to the house, looking around at everything. She came to the wooden fence that went completely around the house where the different colored roses were. She stopped to smell each color. Aunt Susie noticed her smelling the roses from inside the house and came out to greet her.

Sarah said, "These flowers are so beautiful. I could lie in a bed of these roses every night."

Aunt Susie laughed and said, "You're silly today."

She then went over to the pink ones and said, "These are my favorite. They're pink, but the tips are almost red. I love them." Aunt Susie asked Sarah if she wanted to cut a few to put in the house and her bedside. Sarah replied with a big smile, "Oh yes, I would really love that!" Aunt Susie then pulled a small knife out of a pocket in her dress and asked Sarah which roses she would like to cut to take into the house. Sarah said, "Okay, well, I love the yellow and red ones."

"Okay, honey," Aunt Susie took the small knife and cut the stems semi long so that they could trim inside the house. She said to Sarah, "be careful of the thorns. We have to clip them off inside. Okay?" They gathered all the cut flowers and then walked inside the house. The house was so cozy and beautiful; wooden furniture with a thick wool blanket over the arms. The dining table was long like a huge piece of a tree cut in half and sanded smooth. The stove was a cast-iron unit. On top was a pot they called a kettle. They usually heated up water there for cooking or bath water or tea type of drink. She had a few empty glass containers that she used to put flowers in. It looked like she did this often. She mentioned that tonight they're having beef stew with vegetables and cornbread.

Sarah said, "It sure smelled great. I can't wait. I'm so hungry today."

Aunt Susie smiled and said, "Your uncle Ted will enjoy this supper too, it's his favorite." So they continued to cut the roses and clip the thorns off and placed them into the glass containers. Aunt Susie then told Sarah, "Go set one of these by your bed and then one in my room."

"Okay," Sarah answered and got up all excited.

Sarah slowly turned and looked to where she was supposed to take the flowers and noticed two doors down across from the living room.

She opened the door, and a big bed sat up with a white bedspread. It looked so clean and pure; beautiful white bedspread. On her vanity dresser mirror, she noticed a silver brush that looked very similar to the silver mirror Jody found at the dump yard. She sat the glass container next to the silver brush then walked out slowly to the other room. She slowly opened the door and saw a smaller bed with an iron frame, foot, and headboard. The bedspread was a deep-red quilted-type bedspread. Sarah's jaw dropped. It was simple but beautiful. The dresser sat across from the bed between the two windows. In the closet was where all dresses were hanging; brown ones, pink ones, and white ones. On the bottom of the closet were two other types of shoes; black boot-looking shoes and white shoes—leather, buttoned-up, and closed toe. Small shiny embroidery on the sides of the shoes decorated them simply. She then walked over to the vanity and sat down and looked into the mirror. Sarah spoke to herself as she was looking into the mirror and softly whispered, "This place is so different but beautiful. To be the only child, could be so nice. I love Betsy and Aunt Susie and Uncle Ted, they are amazingly sweet. God bless them. I don't know how long we're going to be here, I just don't know. I love my mom and brothers and sisters, but this trip is actually really fun."

Soon, Aunt Susie called and said, "Supper is almost done, can you go call Uncle Ted?"

Sarah said, "Sure." Sarah ran outside to the barn and called Uncle Ted.

Soon, she saw Uncle Ted hanging up a few things and started walking toward the house. He then called out, "Is supper ready?"

Sarah said, "It sure is, it's your favorite."

Ted asked, "Beef stew?"

"Yep! It smells so great in the house, and Aunt Susie made corn bread as well."

"I can't wait," Ted said as he walked up with his arm around Sarah.

Sarah smiled and walked in the same motion. They got to the front door, and he shuffled his feet to make sure he stomped the dust and dirt off. Sarah followed as well. They came in, and Sarah sat down at the table. Uncle Ted went to the washroom to wash his hands and face then, shortly after, came out and sat at the table. Auntie served him a big bowl of stew and corn bread then served Sarah her share and then her share. They all sat, then Uncle Ted said grace. They bowed their heads and then said amen. Then they started eating. The conversation was soft and friendly.

They finished up and then sat their dirty dishes by the sink. Aunt Susie told Sarah to go ahead and get ready for bed and that she'd be in there in a little bit because she had to talk with Uncle Ted.

Sarah said, "Okay," then mentioned that supper was the best supper she's had in a very long time. "It was so delicious, Auntie. Thank you so much, both of you." She then carried on to the bedroom and shut the door. Sarah sat on the end of the bed and took her boots off then looked in the dresser to see if there were different clothes to wear to bed. Sarah just sat there and waited for Susie. Sarah wondered what to do; she felt confused, but happy at the same time. She wondered what tomorrow would bring.

Sarah heard a knock on the door. When she opened, it was Susie. She had the silver brush in her hand. She said to Sarah, "Turn around, and I'll brush your hair, then we'll clip it up for bedtime." They spoke about girl stuff, school, their hair, flowers, and boys. Sarah asked how long Ted and she had been together.

Susie said, "Almost fourteen years, honey." She was so sweet talking. Sarah thought to herself that she wanted to know how her parents died but was scared to ask.

She didn't want to seem like she was a stranger, so Sarah said, "Would you mind talking about my mom and my dad?"

She looked at Sarah and said, "Well, okay, your mom was my sister. She was half Chickasaw Indian, your dad was Caucasian. Your parents weren't married, so your mother was pregnant alone, and during birth, she died, that's how your uncle and I got you. Your mother was so beautiful and smart. She was an artist and had a great sense of humor.

She loved you so much! Your father was never found, but she did mention that she fell in love with him very quickly. He was a cowboy that was riding through the country land and stopped for a few weeks in the small village she was living."

"When was this, Auntie?"

Susie answered, "1515."

"Oh my goshhhhhhhhhh!" Sarah yelled.

It scared Susie and said, "What's the matter?"

Sarah said, "Ohhhhhhh, never mind. Oh my gosh." Sarah kept repeating that over and over to herself.

Then Susie said, "Okay, hand me the clips." Susie clipped Sarah's hair back for bedtime, reached around her with her arms, and said, "I love you very much. Sleep with the angels, Sarah, see you in the morning." Sarah's heart melted instantly. She had wished her mother back home, sat, and brushed her hair or spent time with her like Susie had done today. Sarah laid in her bed and pulled the covers over, and stared at the ceiling, thinking of how different things were here and now than back home. She then turned over to her side and blew out the candle that was sitting on the nightstand beside her. She then rolled back and softly did a few prayers for Aunt Susie and Uncle Ted, her parents, family back home, and her friends who were at strangers' houses tonight.

CHAPTER 13

Jason was called by a woman in town. The lady was a tall lady. She wore a long white dress, tight at the waist and flared at the bottom. She had a big hat on and white gloves. Perhaps she came from money because her attire was very nice, proper, and new looking. Her voice was highpitched and shrill like. Jason instantly felt irritated with her voice and rolled his eyes as she spoke. They walked over to a closed carriage, black in color. The seats inside the carriage were red leather. The driver of the carriage was a slender man with a funny-looking mustache. He wore a black tuxedo-type jacket and a black hat. He didn't smile or talk. He sat up almost on top of the carriage where two horses were attached by harness and chains. The gentleman climbed down the carriage, walked over to the lady, and opened the door on the carriage. He extended out his hand to guide and helped her up and into the carriage.

Jason then followed and sat at the opposite side of the lady. The driver told Jason, "Good day, sir," and tipped his hat. The driver then climbed back up to the top of the carriage then soon heard him yell, "Giddy up, yahhhhh!" Shortly after that, the horses moved in a forward motion gaining speed. Jason braced himself for the ride. It was a bit bumpy. Jason said, "Excuse, ma'am, where are we going."

The lady looked down her nose and said, "You know exactly where we are going, young man."

Jason replied, "No, I don't, ma'am."

She said loudly, "Jason, I don't have time to play games tonight! We're going home, I have things to do!" Jason then scooted close to the window and watched the scenery go by. She continued reading a small book. Jason had a feeling the ride was going to be a little while, so he just kept quiet and watched exactly where they were going. After about ten minutes, Jason saw off to the distance what looked like a large building—square and very large in shape. The building had a tall stone-like fence going all the way around the property which the large building sat on. Trees lined the fence, and bushes were perfectly sculpted in round-type balls. As they got closer, he saw that the building wasn't a building and that it was a very large house. It stood tall with white-painted bricks. It almost looked like the White House. They pulled up to a large two-door iron gate where a man was standing. When we pulled up, he swung open the gates for them then shut them behind after we passed. The driver of the carriage slowly pulled up to the front of the house where a lot of steps led up to the front door. The house was two-story with white pillars supporting the top portion. Jason couldn't believe his eyes. The house looked like a mansion. Soon, the driver of the stagecoach climbed down and opened the door and extended his hand to the lady to help her down the steps and off the coach. Then he said to Jason, "There you go, sir." Jason said thank you and slowly walked behind the lady.

While he was walking up to the door, he was turning himself in circles, awing at everything in the yard. On each side of the steps, which led up to the door, were big potted plants. They lined the walking path. Jason counted each step. He mumbled, "one, two, three, four, five." He counted twelve steps. The lady in front of him opened the door, and a man in a suit took her hat and shawl and her umbrella. She then turned and told Jason to go to his room and do his homework. Jason thought to himself, *Homework?* So Jason started through the door opening in the room, which appeared to be the formal dining room. He couldn't help but turn in circles looking at everything. The windows were so large, and the curtains were golden in color and silk type; they were pulled back by a shiny gold rope with large tassels on the end. They were beautiful. The paintings on the wall were quite large. Jason looked down the halls and thought, *This place is huge.* The floors were a pattern of hardwood flooring. They were so shiny like you could take your shoes off and slide on them. The staircase was slightly spiraled upward to a second level. A lady in a black-and-white dress (which appeared to be a housekeeper or maid) was headed down the steps as Jason was heading up. She was carrying a bucket and mop. She didn't look at Jason, but Jason asked her, "Excuse me, ma'am, could you tell me where my room is?"

She looked at him like she didn't understand. She said softly, "Excuse me, sir?"

He then whispered, "Can you please tell me what room is mine?"

She then pointed to the right of the staircase. "The second door at the right, sir." She answered like she was bothered and scared at the same time. She then scurried down the steps and down the hall. Jason carried on up the staircase then turned right like the housekeeper said. Jason slowly opened the door that led to the room that she mentioned was his. The walls were painted white all throughout the house, but when he got into his room, it was a different story. The room had a tall ceiling with stripe-like wallpaper going from the ceiling down to the halfway where a wall trim (called a chair rail) was followed by wanes paneling on the bottom half of the chair rail trim. There was a tall dresser on one wall, a mirror on another, and two nightstands on each side of the bed. Big lamp-type lanterns were sitting on top of nightstands filled with lantern fuel. The room had a small desk sitting in the corner close to Jason's bed. He also noticed that three animal heads were mounted and displayed on the wall up closer to the ceiling. One was an elk, one was a wild boar, and one was a small mountain lion. Jason couldn't believe this room was his. Jason sat on the edge of the desk and looked through the nightstand to give him a clue that it was his room. He then hopped off the bed and sat on the chair that sat up against the desk and decided to go through the desk. On top of the desk were a fountain pen and an ink jar, plain white paper, and wax with a brass stamp with the letters *J* and *F*. He sat there in awe with what he found. *Who am I?* Jason asked himself.

Jason held his head with confusion. There were books on the desk and a journal of which Jason wrote. Inside the books, it was written in ink, "*Property* of Jason Farrhiss." Soon, the man that greeted him at the door knocked on his door and said, "Here are your clean clothes, sir."

Jason then replied, "Oh, thank you, sir, thank you!" Jason then asked him, "Who is the boss of the house?"

The gentleman said to Jason, "Excuse me, sir, what are you asking me?"

Jason replied, "I know this doesn't make sense of me asking this, but I want to know who is the boss here."

He said softly, "Sir, your parents, Senator George Farrhiss and Mrs. Judy Farrhiss."

"Ohhhhh," Jason replied. "Thank you! Is there anything I can help you with, sir?"

The man (who was apparently the butler) replied with absolutely, "Not, sir."

Jason said to him, "I have just one more question. What is your name and the lady I saw carrying the bucket down the staircase?"

He replied, "We don't go by our first names, but my name is Eugene Barrkins, you can call me Mr. Barrkins, and her name is Ms. Clarice Smitty, you may call her Ms. Smitty."

"Okay, Eugene," Jason answered. Jason said to Mr. Barrkins, "I sure am hungry, when is supper?"

"If you're hungry, sir, I will bring you something to eat."

Jason said, "I can fix it!"

Mr. Barrkins replied very quickly and adamantly, "*Oh*, no, sir, I will bring you a snack!"

"Okay," Jason said, "I greatly appreciate that, I'm so hungry!" After the butler left, Jason decided to venture out and walk around upstairs in a secret manner as if he was not supposed to walk around. He was a little fearful of where he was at the moment. A restroom was located next to his room. It had a sink and a porcelain tub that had brass feet. The toilet was simple, the tank was sitting high up on the wall with a long chain hanging down to pull and flush. Jason then went to the next room, looked around, and out the windows. Each room was decorated very fancily. The rooms were spotless; no clutter, no signs of any other kids. Shortly after, he heard footsteps coming, and he hauled himself down the hall landing area back to his room.

The butler Mr. Barrkins had a small platter that had some grapes, cheese, crackers, and an apple. He set it down on his desk and said, "Is this adequate, sir?"

Jason said, "Sure, this looks great." Jason took the platter to his bed and lay back and snacked on the cheese and crackers then nibbled on the shiny-red apple. As he nibbled on his shiny-red polished apple, he read a few pages of the journal. The journal talked about his dad the senator. Jason thought to himself, *Oh my gosh, I'm the son of a rich man. The senator. How nutty is this?* He read through the journal, and from what he read, he had a very controlled life. He then found the pages that were written about the animals that were displayed in his room. Mr. Farrhiss (Jason's dad) took him on a hunting trip each time. He brought home his game that he killed himself. The senator had the heads mounted and displayed for his son in his room. Jason felt sad that he killed these animals for fun, but that's what men did of these times. Jason rationalized his feelings. He also felt sadness that, back home, he didn't get to spend quality time with his real dad like it seemed in this journal of his dad in this time. Jason could only wish he could be that close with his dad now. He then thought about his mother who was so beautiful and sweet. He missed her greatly and his little sister and little brother.

It was evident that Jason in this time period had no siblings. His heart felt sad at that moment. Jason then closed his eyes and fell asleep. He fell into a deep sleep, so deep he wasn't aware his mother was downstairs and that his father was home and wanted to see him. She called and called. Jason never answered. Soon, Jason was woken up by the shrill, high-pitched voice of a woman who was his mother. She spoke loud and clear, *"Jason! Jason!* Wake up! Your dad is in his office and wants to see you!"

It startled Jason, so he flew off the bed with confusion and said, *"What? What?* Where am I?"

His mother said, "Get downstairs and meet your dad in the office, *now!"* He gathered himself and ran downstairs. As he got down to the bottom of the stairs, he asked the butler, "Where is my dad's office?" He pointed down to the right. Jason walked quickly to the end of the hall to a door to the right. He knocked on the door, and a man's deep voice said, "Enter!" So Jason opened the door and entered very slowly. The man said, "Come in, son, come in!" The man was sitting in a big high-backed leather chair behind a large walnut wood desk. There were stacks and stacks of papers on the desk and on the floor at the base of the desk. He was smoking a pipe similar to Sherlock Holmes's pipe. The room was filled with smoke, which made Jason cough. "Oh, boy, have a seat," the man spoke to Jason.

Jason then spoke softly and said, "Sir, did you want me for something, sir?"

He then said, "Yes, I need you to do me a favor. I need these papers filed into boxes. You can retrieve the boxes that are located in the storage barn. I have three there that you can use. Just walk out to the barn and grab and bring them back in and put these files that are on the ground then take each one back to the storage house."

"Where's that, sir?"

The senator answered, "Oh, boy, you know exactly where that is." Jason felt afraid of upsetting anyone, so he said, "Oh yeah, I forgot." The senator was very tall, over six feet tall, a Caucasian man with shiny jet-black hair. He had a mustache and beard trimmed neatly. He had green piercing eyes with big bushy eyebrows. Jason thought to himself, *This is my dad? Well.* So Jason got up and walked out of the room and out the door located in a short distance, turned right, and walked to the back of the house along a cement trail that led to the backyard and out to a barn-type building. He walked inside the barn and saw the boxes his father was speaking of immediately. He then grabbed three and took them back into his dad's office. He kneeled down and grabbed the papers that were on the ground and neatly filled the boxes until they were full. After he filled them, they were too heavy to carry all at once to the storage, so Jason picked one up at a time and walked out of the office while his dad smoked his pipe and did some paperwork. As Jason walked out of the office, the butler was coming down the hall. Jason whispered for Eugene to come to him. When he did, Jason whispered, "Where is the storage house?"

Mr. Barrkins replied, "Follow me, sir." So Jason followed him across the courtyard area and in a room with a door that was locked with two locks. Mr. Barrkins opened the locks and allowed Jason to set the box down. Jason said, "Thanks, Eugene, I have two more boxes."

Mr. Barrkins said, "Sir, my name is Mr. Barrkins, and I will stand here and wait for you to bring the other boxes."

"Thank you, Eugene," Jason replied, followed by a chuckle. Jason walked back to the office and got the other boxes one at a time, then Mr. Barrkins locked up the door with both locks. Jason then said, "Thank you very much, Eugene," and smiled facetiously. Then Jason headed back to the office and sat back down in the chair in front of his father's desk and swung it around and around and said, "Is there anything else, sir, you'd like me to do for you?"

The senator said, "No, sir, that's all I need right now."

Jason asked him, "What are you writing about, Dad?"

The senator said, "I'm signing some petitions for a political agenda to try to change a few laws."

"Oh," Jason replied, "looks like a lot of work."

The senator replied, "Yes, it is, but it'll be worth it in the long run. One of these days, I'll explain to you what it's all about."

"Okay, sounds good, Dad. May I be excused now, sir?" Jason asked.

"Yes, you may, Jason! Thank you for your help, son."

Jason then got up and exited the office then walked down the large open hall and smelled supper coming from a room that was off to the right through some swinging doors. When he entered through the swinging doors, he saw two women and two men with white aprons on. *Evidently, these people who are my parents of this time have servants and cooks to prepare every meal and event*, Jason thought to himself. So when Jason walked in, he looked at everything that everybody was doing. He said to one of the ladies that was making sausages, "I know how to do that, I do that with my pa back home." The lady looked at Jason like he was talking another language. He said, "The easiest way to do this is if there are two people. A lot of people use a twenty-two-millimeter sheep casing, but my pa uses a twenty-four-millimeter hog casing because he makes Italian sausages." Jason grabbed one of the ends of the casing they were using and said, "Here, you feed it through this manual turner, my pa has an automatic one, and I'll hold the end and just keep pushing through as I hold and twist the sausage to small links." So Jason grabbed the end of the sausage tubing and fed the sausage through. He twisted every three or four inches. He did a whole run and said, "See, I love doing this." Everybody stopped what they were doing and stared at him in awe. In the near distance, he heard his name being called from his "mother" Mrs. Farrhiss. "Oh shoot," he postured, and then hopped around the kitchen island. She then came through the swinging doors of the kitchen and said, *"Jason!"* all loud, "what are you doing here in this kitchen while the help works?"

"Uh, nothing, I thought I left my book in here, so, uh," Jason answered, all awkward and strange.

She replied, "Jason, you've been acting strange all day, you need to go back upstairs and clean yourself up for supper. A few of your father's friends are coming for supper, and I want you to be on your utmost behavior! Do I make myself clear, Mr. Jason Farrhiss?"

Jason slightly smiled and said, "but of coarse mom." Jason had seen plenty of movies to know what kind of people Mrs. Farrhiss was, so Jason acted accordingly. Mrs. Farrhiss turned around and went back out through the swinging doors. Jason followed, but just before he went out of the kitchen, he looked back at the staff and whispered, "Thanks, guys and gals!" and winked. Mrs. Farrhiss stood at the bottom of the stairs and pointed for Jason to go upstairs. The butler Mr. Barrkins was standing right next to her. Mrs. Farrhiss spoke to the butler sternly and said, "Please follow Jason and guide him as to what he is to wear tonight. Help him with his tie and shoes."

"Yes, ma'am," Mr. Barrkins replied. Jason ran up the staircase and to the right to his room and slammed the door. He jumped on the bed and spoke to himself softly, *Where the hell am I? I can't wait to see what this supper is all about.*

The butler knocked and said, "Sir J., I have your bath drawn. Come to the restroom quickly to bathe."

"Okay," Jason replied. He gathered a few things and headed over to the restroom. He undressed and got into the bath and continued with washing his hair and body. He finished quickly then got out and dried off. The butler stood guard, so to speak, outside of the restroom. Jason had a towel wrapped around his waist and walked back over to his bedroom. He first put his underwear on, then undershirt, then socks, then his pants. The butler asked if he needed assistance in anything, and Jason asked, "Yeah, come in, Eugene." The butler stood in straight proper form as Jason put on his white buttoned-up shirt. Jason sat on the edge of the bed and asked Eugene if he liked working here for his parents. He answered yes. Jason then asked, "Are you married, Eugene?" He answered no. Jason asked, "Do you have any children?" Eugene answered no. The butler didn't ask questions or say anything improper. Jason said, "I know you don't understand this, but I'm not exactly who you may think I am."

Mr. Barrkins said, "Sir, it's okay, I am here to do one thing and one thing only, and that's to get you dressed and ready for the supper event." At that moment, Jason figured out that telling him anything else about his real life would not matter either way. Eugene was a very structured professional. He did what Mr. and Mrs. Farrhiss would tell him. Jason finished primping himself and put on his jacket that Mr. Barrkins was holding for him. Mr. Barrkins took a quick onceover at what Jason was wearing: shoes, tie, jacket, and hair.

"You look immaculate, sir," Mr. Barrkins said to Jason.

"Thank you, Mr. Barrkins," Jason replied. Jason then walked out of the bedroom to the landing hall path then started down the stairwell when he noticed a lot of people already gathered around downstairs. The men were dressed in tuxedos, and the women were wearing long dresses with a lot of beading on them.

They almost looked like the curtains hanging on the windows. Jason stopped halfway down the staircase and looked at everybody mingling with one another. Jason didn't see any children like him and became very saddened, and then all of a sudden, he saw a young lady about his age all dressed up. He stared at her while she walked around with her father. She obviously came from money. She floated around like a butterfly. Jason's eyes were taken aback; his heart started racing as he stepped down the rest of the way on the staircase. He then walked into the dining room. The table was long with two candelabra set seperate evenly in the middle of the table. The place setting had white-clothed napkins and a full set of silverware settings at each chair position. There were twenty-two seats at this table. Each setting had name cards placed next to the crystal water glasses, so Jason walked around to find his name and found it and then walked away. He stood at a distance watching the young lady. He didn't know what to say to her, so he just waited for maybe the right moment. Jason wasn't shy, and evidently, his parents here in this time period had many events similar to the one being held at this moment.

Jason decided to walk over to her and introduce himself, so he tapped her on her shoulder and said, "Excuse me, miss. Hi, my name is Jason, what is yours?"

She replied with a slight giggle, "I know who you are, silly."

Jason then said, "You do? Wow! Would you like to take a walk with me? Get away from all these adults?"

She answered, "Sure, Jason, I'd love that." He walked down the hall with her and then asked if she knew where she was sitting.

She said, "No, but I'm sure it'll be right next to my dad."

"Oh, and what is your name?" Jason asked her.

"Oh, it's Milly O'Brian, which you already know because I've been to many of these functions, and you and I always talk."

"I'm sorry." Jason chuckled. "It's a pleasure meeting you, Milly."

She laughed with a slightly strange look on her face. Jason extended his hand out to shake her hand. They then took a walk around the side and at the back of the house. People were spread out enjoying the late afternoon. He asked her what school she attended and if she had any brothers or sisters and where her mom was and how she got so rich. Milly answered Jason and said, "Oh, Jason, you know that I have a younger sister and brother and that my mom passed away several years ago. I come to these functions with my dad because he wants me to get out and meet new people and perhaps pick up the knowledge of politics." Milly said sternly, "I don't like politics, but I have learned a thing or two."

Jason replied, "Yeah, I don't understand all this mumble jumble." They laughed, then about that time, a ring from a metal triangle hanging at the side door rang, which meant that supper was ready to be served. Jason and Milly made their way back to the dining room then watched each other sit down at their place cards, which were directly across from each other. It made Jason smile. Everybody moved in and sat at their place card. Soon, Jason saw his mother and dad enter the dining room, then his mother sat next to him, and his father sat at the head of the table. Soon, water was served, then fine china plates were dealt out to each and every person. The supper consisted of beef slices with au jus, potatoes, vegetables, and a dinner roll. After everybody had their plate, his father stood up and clicked his knife against the crystal glass to get everybody's attention then made a short speech about thanking everybody for coming to the supper and that he hoped that the agenda that he was supporting would be in everybody's interest. He then said a small grace then sat down. He then told everybody to enjoy their food. Everybody ate peacefully. Many finished then started to talk at the table. Jason and Milly started talking about what they were going to do tomorrow. Jason told her that after school, he was going to meet some friends to talk about a trip.

Milly asked, "What kind of trip?"

Jason answered, "Very vague, just a little trip I'd like to take with them someday."

She laughed and said, "It sounds fun." All of the plates were picked up by the servants, then pie was served for dessert. After dessert, Jason and Milly got up and took a walk around the backside, and Jason felt compelled to tell Milly that he wasn't who he was and that he was from 1945 era. Milly thought he had lost his mind because she had known Jason for many years.

He sat Milly down and said, "How would you like to know what's it like in the 1900s?" She humored him and said, "Okay, Jason, go ahead and tell me about 1945."

Jason went on that he and his friends were actually from another part of the country and that they went to school together, and his decent was Italian, and his real parents owned and operated a deli and market. He also told her how they got there and that a witch did a spell on them, and that's how they ended up here. Milly listened with an intention to be serious but thought that Jason just had a creative adventurous mind. It was then when Milly's father called for her. Jason got up and grabbed her hand and said, "Milly, it was so nice to meet you, I wish you could go back home with me so I could show you what a neat life we have there with automobiles and electricity."

Milly replied, "Oh, Jason, you have an amazing mind. Have a safe trip," she giggled and then ended, "I'll see you soon perhaps. Have a great night! Thank you for everything." Jason then kissed her hand. Her face blushed and giggled and did a slight wave and said goodnight. Jason followed her out then walked upstairs to his room and shut the door. Jason took his jacket off and untied his tie while he stood there remembering the whole night. He continued to get undressed and put his T-shirt on to go to bed. He got under the covers and stared at the ceiling and thought how wonderful and pretty Milly was. He thought about the whole night, then his mind flashed over to his mom, dad, brother, and sister back home. He couldn't wait to meet at the barn to go back home. He prayed that everything would go smoothly tomorrow to return back home.

Shortly after, Jason fell asleep. About an hour later, Jason's mother and father came to his room and told him, "Good night, son. We love you."

Chapter 14

The next day came, and all of the kids woke up from where they stayed. They didn't know where the school was, but they all ended up at the schoolhouse around 7:30 a.m. When they got to the schoolhouse, they noticed everyone going into one wooden white-painted building. It had a steep roofline and two swinging doors at the top of the steps. A lady was standing by the doors greeting the children as they stepped into the class. They all saw each other and hugged each other, glad to see a familiar face. They noticed that all the children were all ages five until sixteen. They all filed in and sat down next to one another. The front of the class looked simple with a wooden desk where the teacher sat and a chalkboard type of board. She had her name written on the front chalkboard. Her name was written in beautiful cursive handwriting: "Mrs. Greene" in pink chalk. The teacher was so different than Ms. White or the other teachers. She wore a long dress, hair pinned up, no makeup, and a bonnet-type scarf over her hair. The teacher's personality seemed to be serious. She sat at her desk and asked that they open their writing pad and write down the words that she chose for a spelling bee. So all the kids opened their booklets and wrote the words that she told them. They looked at each other with a dazed type of face. Bobby and Jason said, "I can't wait to go back home where it's normal." The girls didn't say a word. They seemed to be happy and cheerful. Soon, the class took a break for all the kids to play outside. Some went outside, some stayed in the classroom where the teacher was. The four friends went outside and met under a tree.

They sat there talking about how they got there. Bobby asked, "What exactly did we do that made us come back here?"

Jason said, "Well, we had all the items we found at the dump in the box. I had the card and dice, maybe that's the reason because that creepy witch lady said some stuff about the clock and time, and I had the card and dice." Jason said to the friends, "I have that card but no dice."

Jody said, "Maybe we need to find a dice and a watch."

Bobby said, "I have the pocket watch with me."

Everybody looked at him and said, "You do?"

"Yeah, I've had it in my pocket the whole time."

Sarah replied, "I thought you had it in the box with the other stuff of ours."

"Well, Jody did, but Jody grabbed it just before we poofed away. So okay, our plan is to find a dice then, after school, go over to that barn and sit and try to figure out how to make us go back to our home." Mrs. Greene called all the kids back to the classroom to continue class. The four didn't even really pay much attention to what the teacher was saying because they were preoccupied with thinking about getting to the barn after school. A few hours went by, and soon the teacher made an announcement that class was over and to read from the book they all had, the four gathered their belongings and started to walk outside. Bobby went up to ask the teacher if she had some dice that he could borrow, and she answered yes. She went to her desk then pulled them out and handed them to Bobby. They were strangely old-looking wood dice. She made Bobby sign a sheet for borrowing items so she'd remember who had what. Most of the kids borrowed books or erasers and pencils. Bobby grabbed the dice and said, "Thank you very much. I'll return them when I am done." Bobby then flew outside to meet up with the other. So the four of them started walking down the dirt road, talking about each other's stays overnight.

Bobby mentioned how his was a nightmare and how Jason was the senator's son. The girls briefly spoke about theirs and how they really enjoyed the people. Soon, they came upon a few buildings outside of the little town; they still had little ways to walk. They could see over the foothills that the town was near. It was still early afternoon, and they could hardly contain themselves, thinking that they were going to return home and what they are going to do when they get back. So after about twenty minutes, they came into the town from the side. They looked around to make sure the sheriff wasn't around or any of the women that caught them last time. They could see the barn off to the side about one thousand feet away. They scurried down the side of the street, hopping onto the wooden slats of the front of the stores, then started to run full tilt to the barn. "Whew," Bobby said, "that was close, we made it!"

They all smiled then sat down. Jason said, "Here we go. Let's do this." They all grabbed hands and sat there. They looked around while waiting for the wind to pick them up. They closed their eyes in anticipation. "Oh, please, oh, please take us back home." They slowly opened their eyes to see if they had changed back to their original state, but nothing happened, so they let go of each other's hands.

Jody then said, "Maybe if you bring that card out." She asked Jason and Bobby, "Do you guys remember what the old lady said? At all?"

"Uh, not really, it wasn't clear," Jason said. "She said something about time in time, the clock of—I don't know."

Sarah then said, "Jason, pull out the ace card, and Bobby, where's the dice? Put the card in the middle. Oh, where's your pocket watch, Bobby?"

"Right." Bobby searched his pocket. "Oh my god, oh my god, it's not in my pocket!"

"Where did it go?" they all asked. Bobby flew up and looked all panicked, tracing his steps back to the doors of the barn. "Maybe it's outside of the barn, let me go look." So Bobby looked out the doors then said, "Let me look, stay right there." As he stepped out, he saw at the end of the town the man who was his father.

He was riding a horse into town. Bobby ran quickly a few hundred feet looking frantically on the ground. *Where the heck is it?* Bobby started talking to himself. "Please, oh, please help me find my watch," Bobby chanted over and over. And as he hopped over the wooden sidewalk in front of a store, there was a shining beam to his eye. He reached down and grabbed it then turned and started to sprint back to the barn. He saw his dad getting closer, and just as Bobby got to the barn, he heard his dad call out, "Boy! Where are you headed?" Bobby acted like he didn't hear him say anything. Bobby came into the barn running so fast and out of breath. "Hurry, you guys, my dad, that man! The one I was with last night is outside this barn and is coming closer. Hurry! Hurry!" Bobby shouted. "Here's the watch!" Bobby threw it in the middle next to the ace card. They grabbed each other's hands. As they grabbed hands, they all started saying stuff like "It's time to go, it's time to go, the clock is ticking, time to go home." They held hands tightly, saying it over and over. The barn doors opened, and the man yelled, "*Bobby! Boy! What are* you doing? Come here!"

Just about that time, the wind picked up. They started yelling the words, "Time to go, time to go, clock is ticking, time to go back home!" The wind picked up so strong that it was throwing dirt and hay all around. They could hear the man saying, "Hey, Bobby! Get over here now!" The man started walking closer, but the wind was whirling around so fiercely, then Jason let go of Jody's hand but continued to hold Bobby's and threw the dice. When Jason threw the dice, a circle of smoke circled them, and poof! They banished in midair. The man looked around all confused. He couldn't believe what he just saw. He turned around and around and called out for Bobby. While looking around, the wind died down, and the dust started to settle. He was so confused at the event. He sat down on the bale of hay stacked next to others. He took his hat off and rubbed his hands over his eyes.

CHAPTER 15

The kids had disappeared from the barn and returned back to the baseball field. As they held hands and their eyes tight, the wind died down, and they all opened their eyes. They immediately looked around and noticed one of the kids didn't return. Their hearts started beating so fast. "What? What happened, where's Jody? Jody didn't return with us? *How? Why? What?* Sarah said and instantly started to cry.

Bobby said while tears started to roll down his dirty face, "Where's Jody? We have to go back and get her. We just do. I don't know how to?"

"I'm scared too," Jason added.

"What do you mean, Jason?" Bobby frantically asked. "There are no questions, we have to go back! We just have to." Bobby put his face on his hands and started to cry.

Jason had tears whaling up in his dark eyes. "Okay, you guys, let's perfect this time traveling thingy." Bobby wiped his face as Sarah did. Jason said, "Maybe we should go home then do this tomorrow, it's getting dark here. I don't even know how long we've been gone. Has it been a full day or several days? Let's find this all out and come tomorrow and figure it all out." Sarah grabbed her necklace. Jason grabbed the box and the clock, and Bobby grabbed his watch. They grabbed the bikes.

Sarah said, "Do we leave Jody's bike, or should I take it?"

The boys said, "Maybe take it, but what am I gonna tell everybody that would ask?"

"I don't know. Maybe that we don't know where Jody is? Oh my gosh, if she doesn't come home tonight, the police will be out looking for her, her grandma is going to be so devastated. I don't like this one bit," Bobby said. So they decided to take her bike and ride it almost to Jody's house and leave it on the side, then Sarah walked the rest of the way home. Bobby took Jason to his house then hauled off to home. Bobby pedaled so fast and hard. He finally got home. He walked in the door, and his mom was in the kitchen putting supper together. He walked right up to her and gave her a big hug. His mother looked at him and asked, "What's wrong, Bobby?"

Bobby looked at her and said, "I sure do love you and Dad."

She laughed and said, "We love you too, Bobby. What's wrong?"

"Nothing, Mom, I'm just so tired, I need to lie down for a little bit, call me when supper is ready."

"Okay, son, I'll let you know. Your father will be home in an hour or so."

When Jason returned home, he walked in from the back after he put the golden box away in the garage. He walked up and saw his mom on the service porch putting some laundry into the washer. He walked in and could smell the Italian food cooking. It was the best smell ever. His heart felt comfortable and happy that he was finally home. One day and a night in 1515 seemed like a lifetime. He hugged his mom and told her that he loved her.

She said, "I love you too, Jason. How was your day?"

He said, "Tiring. Where's little brother and sister?"

"Oh, they're in their room, son."

"Okay, I'll go check on them. I want to lie down for a little bit before Papa gets home."

"Okay, son," his mother answered. All Jason could think of was Jody. That Jody didn't come back with them. He looked in on the little brother and sister and picked them up and swung them around and gave them kisses on their forehead and told them that he loved them then sat them back down and walked into his room and shut the door. He laid face down on his bed and took a big whiff of the blanket and felt the pillows then started to cry into his pillow that they left Jody behind. Jason spoke to himself softly and said, "I had to let go of her hand to roll the dice. I didn't do this, right? How could she stay behind? I can't believe this." Jason wiped his tears into his pillow then shortly fell asleep. He felt so tired, it was like he was pulled through the wringer and back.

Sarah got home; she went inside, and her mom was in the bathroom washing the floor. Sarah marched in there and said, "Mama, te amo!" which means in English, I Love you". Sarah hugged her while she was on her knee's cleaning.

Her mom said with worry, "Mi Amor" which means in English "my love", what's wrong?"

Sarah replied, "Nothing, Mama. I'm just tired. I may be coming down with a cold. I don't know. Would it be okay to go lie down for a while?"

Her mom answered, "Yes, dear. Supper is in the oven, so not much has to be done tonight."

Sarah went to her room and laid down. She grabbed the stuffed doll that she got for her tenth birthday and hugged it tight and started to cry for Jody. "Oh, Jody, I pray that you're okay." Sarah felt so sad that her best friend didn't return with her. She was so worried that her grandma would be devastated. Soon, Sarah fell asleep.

CHAPTER 16

Back at the barn, the man that was Bobby's dad still sat on the bale of hay in dissolution. He put his hat on and then noticed a young girl standing at the barn doors looking out. He said, "Excuse me, little miss, what are you doing?"

She answered, "Oh, just waiting for my ma, she's supposed to be picking me up here in a little bit."

He then asked her, "Where did your friends go? Where did Bobby go?"

"I don't know, sir, we were here, but I thought when the wind picked up that they ran out? I don't know, the wind got so bad, I don't know what happened." Jody knew exactly what happened when they had been saying the chant and held hands and when Jason let go to roll the dice. At that split second, Jody undid her hand from Sarah. Jody decided at that particular moment that she wanted to live in the 1500s because she had the family that she had always wanted, a mother, father, and two beautiful sisters—a perfectly happy life. Jody did feel sad for her grandmother. In fact, tears rolled down Jody's face when she thought of it but thought that she'd have a fuller life there in the little country town where her new ma and pa and sisters lived. She couldn't wait to get back home to hold Ellie and talk with her mom and older sister. It was something Jody wanted her whole life, and now, she had it. Soon, Jody saw her new mom and the girls walking from store to store in the town. Jody opened the barn doors and ran over to them and immediately fit in like a piece of a puzzle. She grabbed Ellie the baby, and they continued to walk through the stores with their mom.

CHAPTER 17

Back in Kalamazoo, Michigan, 1945, the three of the friends ended up taking naps. They all woke up in dismay and sadness but grateful that they were able to get back home safe and sound. Each of them couldn't wait for the morning to come to talk to each other about what they had gone through. It was so amazing and unimaginable and scary at the same time. Jason sat in his room looking at the clock's detail, opening the drawer looking slowly at every detail. He rubbed his fingers over the carvings and sculpture details of the front and sides of it. He thought to himself, *Where did this clock really come from? Why does it have this power? Whose engraved initials were on the back?* "These are the things that we need to figure out," Jason whispered out. He still had the card in his pocket and the wooden dice that Bobby got from the teacher back in 1515, but Jason also had the dice that he initially threw at the baseball field.

Jason opened his notebook pad and started writing details down, date, time, what was said, where they traveled to, the year, etc. He figured that details were very important to go back in time to get Jody and bring her home. His mother called him for supper, so it interrupted his writing, but this is one dinner that he didn't want to miss. He missed everything about home, even though he wasn't rich like he was in 1515. Jason closed his book then ran down the hall to the kitchen and asked his mother if she needed help. She replied, "No, Jason, thank you though for asking. Go ahead, sit down, Jason, your dad is in the restroom and will be here in a few minutes."

"Okay," Jason eagerly replied. He walked by his little sister and gave her a kiss on her head and then asked his little brother to sit by him. The little brother came and hopped up on the chair next to him. Jason reached over and scuffed his head with his knuckles and whispered to him, "You're a good kid, you know that, Richie." Shortly after, he saw his dad walk out from the restroom, and Jason flew up out of his chair from sitting and ran to his pa and gave him a great big tight hug. "Pa, how are you doing?"

Jason's dad laughed and said, "I'm good, son, good!" His dad asked, "You doing good? Any problems? How's school?"

Jason replied, "Everything is good, Pa! Love you!"

His dad looked strangely, tilting his head and raising his big bushy eyebrows then answered, *"I love you too, Jason!* Now let's have a seat and enjoy your mom's delicious cooking." Jason's mom came out and sat three large dishes in the middle of the supper table. She had made Jason's favorite: rigatoni with meatballs and melted cheese and also Jason's dad's favorite dish *lasagna al forno*. They all blessed their food and each other. Jason had his own little thought and prayer for Jody. They all said amen then started to pass things around to eat. The night grew later. Jason went to bed feeling anxious about the thought of traveling back to 1515. His thoughts got so overwhelming that he closed his eyes then fell asleep.

CHAPTER 18

Bobby and Sarah's supper was very similar to Jason's. They felt so grateful to have the family they had and were thankful for their parents. Although Sarah felt grateful, she had a small thought of a memory of the family she was with in 1515. Her aunt and uncle were so great there. Sarah felt sad for leaving them behind and felt anxious when her papa came home from work. He was always so angry speaking. Soon, after finishing up her dinner, she asked to help clean up the dinner and started to wash the dishes. Usually, the father would ask her or the girls to hop to it. Her father spoke only Spanish with them.

Sarah finished up the dishes and asked if it would be okay to go to bed and that she felt very tired. She kissed her father on the cheek and then kissed her mama and said, "I love you both very much, goodnight." Sarah walked to her room and got ready for bed. All she could think of was her best friend Jody and how she was doing and feeling and how her grandma was handling not having her around.

Sarah felt a deep pain in the pit of her stomach when she thought of how heartbroken Jody's grandma was feeling. Sarah got ready for bed then knelt down on her knees at the side of her bed and interlocked her hands together, squeezing tight. Sarah closed her eyes and started saying prayers over and over for Jody and her grandma. Sarah then got up and grabbed her special stuffed animal, hugged it, and pulled the covers over her head and instantly fell asleep.

CHAPTER 19

At Bobby's house, he helped his mom set the table and brought the food to the dinner table for supper. His father came home, and they all told funny stories about when they were younger. Bobby laughed as to just humor his parents but felt so grateful that he was home with his parents. Bobby felt like he was in a fog and only heard some stuff his parents were talking about. Bobby finished up supper before his parents did then asked if he could help with the dishes or anything. They both replied quickly and said, "Thank you, Bobby, for asking, but we got it."

He then walked over to both of them and gave them a big hug and kissed them on the cheeks and said, "I'm so grateful for having you both as my parents. I love you so much." Tears whaled up in Bobby's mom's eyes, and his dad's face had a proud kind of shocking look upon it. Bobby then turned and said, "Good night, I'll see you tomorrow, "Bobby went to his room, shut the door, and laid down on his bed, then started to think about Jody. Tears rolled down his face like a faucet had been turned on. He whispered to himself and said, *We'll come back to get you, Jody, just hang on one more day.* Bobby kept praying over and over for her and finally fell asleep.

CHAPTER 20

The next morning came. They all got up, got ready for school, then walked to their bus stop. Shortly, each of them picked up and walked to the back of the bus where they always sat. They just looked at each other and didn't say anything. Their faces were so sad, and when they didn't see Jody come and sit at her seat, they felt even sadder. The bus stopped by Jody's stop, and a girl was standing there waiting. She hopped on the bus and walked all the way to the back and sat right down where Jody would have sat. The three of them got upset and said that their friend Jody sat there. The girl answered, "I know, I'm sitting here!"

Sarah said, "No! That's Jody's seat."

The girl answered all angry looking and said, "*I know*! My name is *Jody*, and I'm sitting where I always sit." It took Sarah, Jason, and Bobby back. Their jaws dropped at the same time. For that split second, they thought, *Oh my gosh, is that you, Jody?* They wanted to say that, but words couldn't come out of their mouths, so they all sat back in their seats as the bus continued driving. It pulled up to the front of the school and stopped. The bus driver opened the door, and all the kids started piling off and walked to their first class. That new girl walked off the bus as the other three walked shortly behind her. They couldn't believe what happened. They had never seen this girl anywhere, so they followed her to see what and where she was going and doing. They had this curious-upset look on their faces as they watched her go into their first class with Ms. White. They watched where she sat. "Oh my god!" Bobby yelled out, and everybody turned. *That girl is sitting on Jody's seat!* Bobby, Jason, and Sarah thought to themselves. They covered their mouths as they sat in their seats. They then turned and faced forward when Ms. White came into the room and started talking. The three kept looking over at the new girl then up at Ms. White waiting for the teacher to announce a new student.

They kept waiting and waiting, and nothing happened, so Ms. White started doing the roll call just about that time the new girl got up and nodded to the teacher as she left. The three had looked at each other and were confused, "What's going on, who was that?" They whispered to each other. Soon, Ms. White had mentioned that they'll be going over to the cafeteria to listen to a speaker for the rest of the class period and the next class's time as well, so they all got up and formed a line to exit the room behind Ms. White. Bobby said to Jason and Sarah, "After class, we go home and get the items to go back and get Jody."

Things just aren't right around here without Jody, and everything seemed out of whack. Sarah agreed, "Yes, after class, we'll ride the bus home then gather our items."

"I'll just walk back to the baseball field," Jason said.

"I'll walk with you, Sarah," Bobby said, "I'll be bringing my bike, you guys."

"Okay. I hope the day goes by faster because I really don't want to be here." Jason ended while they filed into the cafeteria and sat in the chairs that were in rows of thirty. It seemed like the whole school was attending this meeting with a special guest speaker. The special event lasted for two hrs. All the kids were released to a recess then expected to go to their third class. After their third class was lunchbreak. The three of them met and figured out exactly what they were going to do right after class. They picked at their food as if they were in a daze. After an hour, the bell rang to end lunchbreak. Everybody went their separate ways back to their classes. The day couldn't be over quick enough. All of them watched the clock, hoping that school was close to being out. The time lagged on through the day but finally reached 2:45 p.m.

The bell rang, and kids ran out of their classes and to their lockers. Doors swung open, clunking loudly. The three gathered all their items and ran to the bus, hopped on, and headed back to where they always sat. The bus started to pull away, and the three noticed that Jody's seat was empty. They all looked outside to see if that girl was coming but noticed her being picked up by Jody's grandma. The three thought, *Who was that? A cousin? It didn't make any sense. The cops didn't come to school, they weren't searching, why?* But the three of them didn't want to waste their energy on that until they brought Jody back; that was their main focus. The bus went to their bus stops and dropped them all. They ran off to their homes to grab the items. About half an hour, Sarah started walking toward the baseball field. She got down the street, and Jason joined Sarah. They walked quickly, then as they were getting to the field off to the distance, they noticed Bobby riding his bike. They walked over to their spot and sat down. Bobby rode his bike right on the grass to the spot Jason and Sarah sitting, and he threw his bike down and sat down with his pocket watch. As they sat around, they pulled out their items and sat them in the middle. Jason grabbed the clock and sat it in the middle and placed the ace card up and had the dice in his hands.

Sarah took the necklace off her neck and draped it over the clock, and Bobby sat the pocket watch on top of the clock and grabbed Sarah's hand. Jason said "Okay, I don't know what was said, but let's grab hands and chant, "Time, oh, time, it's time to travel, the clock has struck the time to go, to go to Jody in 1515." As they chanted this over and over, they fell into a deep concentration. Their bodies were swaying, and they closed their eyes. Jason threw the dice, and they held each other's hands and repeated the words, "It's time, it's time." They slowly opened their eyes and noticed that nothing was happening, so they stopped what they were doing and let go of each other's hands.

Tears started to fall down Sarah's face. "We have to figure this out, we just have to."

So Jason yelled out at the old lady, "You better take us back to Jody!" Jason placed the ace card on top of the clock, opened the drawer, and started chanting, "It's time, it's time, the clock has struck, it's time." Bobby and Sarah joined in the chant. As soon as they started, they grabbed each other's hands, then they could feel a slight breeze. As they felt the breeze, they said, "This is it, keep saying the words." The wind picked up to a fast whirlwind. The grass and dirt were circling around the three of them. The wind got so high that they could barely hear each other yell, "It's time, it's time." Jason released his hand and threw the dice as Sarah held on to his shoulder. The dice flipped up high, and a six first landed, then the second dice hit and bounced around then off the side of the clock and tipped to a six, and at that second moment in time, a white puff of smoke surrounded them and banished them.

CHAPTER 21

They all opened their eyes and noticed that they were in the middle of a park. Off to the side of the park were cars parked like dominoes. They rubbed their eyes in dismay. "This isn't 1515 in Kalamazoo, Michigan!" Bobby yelled.

"What did you roll, Bobby?" asked Jason. "What did you roll!" Jason answered, "a twelve. I rolled two sixes. It doesn't make sense, all the cars look so different than ours at home, almost like spaceships.

"Where are we?" Sarah's voice cracked. "Oh my god, Jody's not going to be here, she's in 1515. Let's grab our items and go find a newspaper or something and see what time it is, where we are, and what year we are in." They gathered their stuff and started walking across the park. They ended up over toward some buildings that were off to the distance. They could tell it was very futuristic by looking at the automobiles driving around. They couldn't believe where they were. The people wore different types of clothes, and there was a big diversity of people. It seemed to be overpopulated with people. There were so many people walking on the side of the buildings and automobiles driving around. The traffic lights were displayed horizontally from side to side. They also had a blue light displayed instead of just the basic normal red, yellow, and green. Most of the buildings looked either slender tall or like triangular pyramid shaped with lots of chrome and glass. Palm trees and a mixture of cactus-type plants landscaped the town.

There were concrete sidewalks connecting around each of the buildings, and the bicycles even looked different. The bicycles sat short to the ground in a sitting position with no handlebars. Some people were also moving along in a two-wheel motor contraption that you stand on. It kind of looked like a podium metal capsule-looking thing. The three kids couldn't stop staring at the people and things. They sat down right on the sidewalk against a building; they were in so much shock. Their jaws stayed open the whole time as they sat there staring at all the activity that was taking place. Jason thought to himself, *This looks a lot like New York.*

Jason mumbled to himself and asked, "Is this New York?"

Sarah heard Jason and said, "Noo!"

CHAPTER 22

After about twenty minutes of staring at people, they got up from sitting and started walking down the street. They came upon a store called Ralph's. Outside the store were metal shopping baskets and people pushing them. "Looks like maybe it could be a grocery store," Bobby mumbled. The kids walked through the automatic doors that scared them because they had never seen automatic doors. So they hopped back off the black rubber walk path of the automatic doors and waited for people to walk through first. They then followed when people went through it. It was a grocery store; a grocery store that was amazing. Racks after racks of canned goods and a whole aisle of bread selections. "Oh my gosh!" Sarah yelled out. "Look at all the fruit and vegetables! There are tons of it. Oh my gosh, oranges, bananas, apples, and watermelon, every fruit you could think of."

They followed through, and Jason couldn't believe the butcher counter and the cold storages for all the cut meat that were already packaged. Jason picked up some Italian sausage that was already packaged, and he looked at the price per pound, and it said it was $5.45 per pound! Jason repeated that price out loud and said, "Can you believe it, guys? Look at how much this is, oh my gosh, I can't wait to tell my pa! Oh wait, there is no way my pa would believe that we traveled into the future, no way! Man, I wish I had a camera." They walked around the supermarket with a stunned look. They came across a newspaper stand and picked one up, and on the front was a picture of the president shaking hands with someone else. They all put their hands over their mouth and read that the president of The United States was a woman of ethnicity Tessy B. Houstan.

"Oh my gosh, a woman president?" they whispered.

Sarah yelled softly to Bobby, "Find the date, find the date."

As they searched around the first page, they found it hiding, so to speak. It said it's Thursday, October 2053. Bobby put his head down toward his knees with disappointment and confusion. "I can't believe this. We are in the future and in Los Angeles, California, nowhere near Jody." Jason was puzzled and thought to himself, *I want to save this paper or a piece of it, but how do I do this and not get into trouble?* because they didn't have any money to buy the paper, which was $2.50 a copy. So he told Bobby and Sarah to circle around, and he was gonna rip the front page off. Well, right when he started to rip, the manager saw them and yelled out, "Hey! Come back here and pay for that." They all started running out of the store and through the automatic doors and down the street. "Oh my gosh, you guys hurry, run!" So they continued to run down the sidewalk over a few blocks. As they came around the corner, they saw some guys wearing black clothing.

CHAPTER 23

The guys had their hairs slicked back with dark sunglasses on. Jason and Bobby instantly felt a little uneasy. As the guys started walking toward them, they looked so angry like they were pissed off at the three of them. Jason, right off the bat, said, "Hey, can we ask you a question?"

One said, "No!"

The other said, "What's your problem?"

The other guy said, "You need to stay on your side of the town or you're going to get hurt!"

Jason and Bobby explained, "Well, excuse us, we don't understand, we're not from here."

The one in the middle replied, "So what did you want, troll?"

Jason replied, "Troll? My name is Jason, and we're looking for a library. Do you know where one is?"

The guys laughed at Jason and said, "Oh, sure, guys, we know where the library is exactly. Just follow this street to the stop sign then turn right, go halfway down, and it'll be on the right." The three guys laughed and continued walking on, looking back, and laughing. So Jason, Bobby, and Sarah carried on like they had said. As they're walking, they noticed that it doesn't look like a library would be around there; it was an alley. They told them to turn down this way, and when they came upon the direction of the destination, it was a chain-link fence with three very large vicious-looking dogs. The dogs were spitting and drooling saliva while barking and growling as they all were jumping at the fence. They scared them so bad that they started to run all crazy fast away from that sight in the opposite direction that those guys were and kept running. They ran so far from where they were; they lost their sense of directions of where the park was.

CHAPTER 24

They turned the corner and down a residential street, and off to the distance, they saw some large white letters displayed on a hill. All they could read was "wood." Sarah asked the boys, "Wonder what that says on the hill, and why?"

They both replied, "Let's walk a little further and see what it says." As they got further down the street, they noticed in front of *W* was an *L*, *L*, and *Y*. They continued until they could read all the letters, and it finally read "Hollywood." "*Oh my gosh, Bobby and Sarah!* This is the place where actors come and are in movies. I've heard my mom and Pa talk about Frank Sinatra, Lucille Ball, Carey Grant, and John Wayne. Oh my gosh, we're in Hollywood, California. I wonder if we're close to where there's the Hall of Fame star walk and the Chinese Theatre. This is so amazing! I can't believe this," Jason mumbled. "We have to ask somebody how to get there and to the park as well. I don't remember even a name on the park, do you guys?" Jason asked Bobby and Sarah.

Bobby said, "Wait a minute, I did notice off to the distance something like Ekin or Etchon?"

Sarah blurted out, "Echo Park, that's it."

Bobby yelled, "Echo Park!"

"Okay," Jason added, "after we check the stars on the sidewalk, we'll go back over to the park." So they walked over to a man washing his car and asked how far away were the stars on the sidewalk. The guy answered, "It's just up the way about two miles."

The kids nodded and said, "Thank you, sir." They continued on their walk in the direction the man had told them, looking with excited and shocked faces at all the different-looking cars and people's fashions. Jason said to Bobby and Sarah, "Do you guys believe that by this time in our years that we'll be over a hundred years old? So to be here now is only a dream."

"I know," Sarah said, "I can't believe we're here. My family would have never traveled here to see this." As they continued walking, they could see that the town had businesses lined up one after the other on each side of the street. All they could think was that they wished they had some money to spend and that they wished their families could be there to experience all of this too.

CHAPTER 25

They continued to walk down looking at the sidewalk; they had finally hit their first star. It was so amazing! "Oh my gosh, we found it, oh my gosh, you guys," Jason yelled, "look at the star!" The sidewalk was concrete, and in the center is a five-pointed terrazzo and brass star where the actor's, musician's, or director's and producer's names are located in the center. The actors were located randomly, some say that some were located exactly where the actor or awardee wanted. Sarah blurted out all excited, "Maybe we'll see someone famous here." As they continued down the sidewalk, they noticed the famous Chinese Theatre, and in front of the theater were footprints imprinted in the concrete where the famous star would sign their names. Sarah ran over and saw Marilyn Monroe's footprints and put her feet in her impression. "Wow, I'm almost the same size as Marilyn Monroe's feet. Hey, here's John Wayne's, guys."

"Look how big his boots were," Bobby added.

"Oh my gosh, here's Elvis. I can't believe Elvis was right here and signed this concrete and put his feet in the wet concrete." Jason plopped down and just stared at the concrete square. "This is so amazing, you guys, I can't believe this all." Sarah and Bobby ran and hopped over to all the squares, calling out the names.

"Frank Sinatra, Jason!" Bobby yelled!

Sarah yelled, "Lucille Ball!"

Jason yelled out, "Alfred Hitchcock!"

The three of them spun around and around with excitement and amazement. They tried to enter the Chinese Theatre, but a man who worked there stopped them and asked for a ticket. Bobby asked how much the tickets were to see a film, and the guy replied $10.00 a person to see a movie. The three of them turned around and walked away with their heads down. As they were walking away, they decided to walk down the side of the building and noticed a door open. Jason whispered, "Let's go in, guys!"

Sarah hesitated and said, "No, Jason."

Bobby said, "C'mon, let's go in. If they say anything, we'll run out." So they sneaked in the side and walked up some steps then opened the door slowly at the top of the stairs to make sure there was nobody standing by. They peeked through and saw that the restrooms were located near, so Sarah said, "I have to use the restroom," and ran over to the woman's restroom and saw that it was soooo beautiful in there. Mirrors everywhere, it was Victorian decorated, flower-striped wallpaper, and a couch was in there too. Everything was painted white. Sarah sat at the mirrors and looked at herself in a daze, almost as if she was looking through herself. Women walked by and said hi. They were mostly dressed in jeans and a T-shirt, very different from home of her time that she was used to. Sarah sat at the mirrors for a good five minutes just staring at things then went to use the restroom, came out, and washed her hands and dried them then walked out, and Jason and Bobby were waiting.

Bobby said all excited, "Did you see how fancy the bathrooms were?"

Sarah replied, "I sure did, it was beautiful!"

Jason then said, "Hey, let's go into the movie and see what's playing." They entered, and it was dark. The movie was already playing, so they made their way up to the middle front. There weren't too many people in there for the size of the theater. Jason mumbled, "This theater is huge, you guys. No wonder it cost $10 to get in."

"Back at home, we could get in the movies and buy a soda pop and popcorn for a dollar," Bobby whispered. As they sat and watched the movie, they couldn't believe how clear and bright the movie was. The movie playing was Wonder Woman's Return. "Can you believe it, guys?" Bobby blurted out.

Sarah shushed him. "I know, but this is a comic book story that's made into a movie, can you believe it, Jason?"

"No," Jason answered. "Now shush," he told Bobby. They sat back in awe watching the amazing film.

"How did they make her run so fast and fly, and it looked so real when the enemy shot at her," Bobby whispered. They sat for the entire movie then waited for everyone to exit. When the three of them got up, they looked around at the Chinese Theatre's beauty. The red velvet curtains draped from the ceiling down, and the seats were dark stained wood that looked like they were of early times with gold accent and velvet on the arms and back of seats. The moldings up high had accents of gold with a large chandelier at the center of the theater. It was apparent that they had several different types of shows at this theater like operas and magic shows. They had a balcony-like seating way up high which sat approximately ten people per balcony booth. As the kids looked around, they slowly walked up to the back of the theater to walk out. They got to the doors, and the guy that first spoke to Bobby asking for his ticket said, "*Hey*, how did you guys get in here?"

Jason spoke quickly, "We paid."

He then said, "No, you didn't! I was at the door the whole time." They then turned and started running through the rows of seats over and down to an opening through the side. The guy was yelling, "Come back here!" The kids then flew down the side where the bathrooms were through a door down the steps that they first came up and out the door that led to the side of the building. They continued to run out the front and turned quickly on the sidewalk.

CHAPTER 26

"Oh my gosh!" Sarah yelled, look at all the people. Busloads were pulling up and dropping people off at the curb. They couldn't believe their eyes. Off to a little distance approximately five hundred feet, they could see the theater ticket guy looking for them. They continued walking at a fast pace forward then crossed the street to go into a store so that they could ask where the park was located. When they got across the street, they noticed Elvis performing. "Oh my gosh," Jason said, "I'm confused, is this the real Elvis? How could this be." As they stepped closer, they noticed he wasn't really singing and that he just had the music playing from a stereo and danced just like "the king." A little bit further up, they saw a guy named Michael.

"Who's Michael Jackson?" Bobby asked.

"Oh my gosh!" Sarah yelled. "Look up there, Marilyn Monroe, she's so beautiful!"

"That's not her!" Bobby shouted to Sarah. Wow, all these people are performing like the originals. We should just sit and wait a little and watch. So they sat down against the wall of a store that sold souvenirs and watched the performers perform. Then as they were sitting there, they saw a long type of car; people were calling it a limo. It drove up, and a few vans and cameramen hopped out. They sat up their lights and camera equipment in front of the Chinese Theatre, so all three of them stood up to see what was taking place. The police showed up to block off areas. The cop cars looked so different than the ones back home. Long-like miniature buses, sleek slim, and very aerodynamic.

Dark windows and the whole top of the vehicle had red and blue lights, and when they were on, they operated up and down the length of the whole vehicle instead of stationary on the top center of the police car. The three of them stood with anticipation to see who was being honored and why. Shortly after, a woman stepped out of the car and walked up to the center area of the camera and lights. They wondered who it was and why she's there. Where they stood, they noticed more and more people started to crowd close and waited for the presentation.

Bobby asked, "Do you know what's going on?"

A guy answered, "Oh yes, it's Katy Perry."

"Who's Katy Perry, and why is she here?"

The guy said, "You know her! She's that music artist that has made more number one hits than any female artist, so they're adding details to her star."

Bobby replied, "She looks kind of old."

The man replied, "Yeah, she is now, but she made a CD when she was sixty, and it rocked the charts."

"*CD!* What's a CD?" Jason asked.

"That's what music is downloaded on."

"Downloaded?" Sarah asked.

"You know," the guy said, "computer-generated. They used to look like a little record. Small in shape around four inches in circumference, but now, the CDs are only two inches in size."

"We don't have computers, are they robots?"

"Well, sort of."

The guys said, "Yeah, well, look at your phones. You guys must have a cell phone?" he asked.

Jason blurted out, "*What the heck!* A cell phone. You can call at any time and carry it, and people can call you?"

The guy had a strange look on his face and seemed to have gotten irritated with all their questions.

He then replied, "I'm not a fool, guys. You're asking me these questions like you don't know anything. See you later! *Peace!*"

Sarah asked the guys, "Wonder why he got so mad, we were just wondering." So they stood and watched for a little bit then carried on down the street.

CHAPTER 27

"Oh my gosh, you guys, look at the people standing in a line formation. They're moving forward but not walking. How is that?" So they crossed the street then watched how people got on the moving sidewalk then hopped on for the ride. "This is out of this world, guys!" Bobby shouted softly.

Jason said, "Look, it's on both sides, people on the other side are going the opposite direction. This moving sidewalk is going so fast, almost as fast as the cars. Hey, do you guys notice the cars sound different?"

"Yeah," Sarah replied. "I thought that it sounded more quiet than usual, and I haven't noticed a gas station."

"I've seen a store-like place and cars pulling up to something and plugging in. Wonder what they're doing there," Bobby added.

"Let's go see, guys, then we can ask where that park is located. I wonder if we could get some water, I'm so thirsty!" So the three of them got off the moving sidewalk and ran over to where the cars were plugging in. As they got to the store, they read the signs. They read, "To avoid electrocution, please do not drink or spray water in this area." Another sign said, "Allow ten minutes of time when plugging in to charge your electrical mobile."

"What the heck!" Bobby Yelled. "That's so unreal that all the cars are electric. No wonder there's no sound or smell of gas or smoke." So after they read the signs and watched people pull up in their electric cars, they walked into the store to ask for directions and noticed that there wasn't anybody working at the counter. In fact there, wasn't even a counter; there was a slot where people put a card in and it returned it, then the people walked out, plugged their cars in, and inserted the card into a slot. The machine then returned the card, then a green light would light up and start charging. When it was finished, a bell buzzer would ring, and a red light would flash. Inside this store were items to drink and eat, but to obtain any of those, you had to insert either cash or a plastic card, which they heard people refer to it as a credit card. Everything was in a vending machine. The three of them felt like they were in space. Nobody was overly friendly, everybody seemed to be in a hurry; a completely different scene than they were used to. Back home, everybody was friendly and would offer help, much different than here. Just about that time, they all said, "Let's get out of here."

Sarah said, "I miss Jody."

Bobby put his arm around Sarah and said, "I know, I miss her too!"

CHAPTER 28

So they walked over to a person that was charging their car and asked where Echo Park was located. The guy replied, "Just get in, and I'll take you there, I'm going right by there." They all hesitated and looked at each other. Should they trust going with him? He looked younger in his mid-twenties and friendlier than anybody they came into contact with. So they jumped into the car and noticed how futuristic it looked. The guy unplugged his car then hopped in the driver's seat and started the car up. It was so quiet that you couldn't even tell if it had been started or not, but as soon as he did, the whole console lit up like a Christmas tree. It was displayed like a spaceship; all digital readings, red, green, and blue markings. His stereo was so loud that they felt the beat in their chests. The guy asked if they liked the music and buckled up his seat belt and then yelled out, "Buckle up, kids!" The guy said, "Hi, my name is Jeremy, oh, I love this song, isn't it fabulous! "He started dancing in his seat throwing up his hands like he was having a party all by himself. He swung one arm up and around like he was lassoing up a cattle. The kids got so terrified, and they grabbed their seat belt and bowed their heads. Jason sat in the front passenger side. The guy noticed their heads down and turned the music down and laughed. "Are you guys okay?"

Jason looked up and said, "Yeah, we're okay, we're just from the country, not used to all this technology and music."

"Oh," the guy replied, "no problem, I'll get you to the park safely, but we got to get on the Fway."

Jason asked, "What's the Fway?"

"Freeway, you know, where there's a lot of lanes. It's totally faster than taking all the business streets. Just hold tight, we're getting on now."

Jason looked over at how fast he was going but didn't understand the numbers displayed. Something Km/h instead of MPH. Jason thought to himself, *I remember Pa saying that mph means miles per hour.* "So what does Km/h mean, Jeremy?"

Jeremy replied with, "You know, kilometer per hour. Everything is measured in kilometers."

"Oh, okay." Jason sat back as Jeremy got on the Fway. He accelerated to 180 kilometers per hour, which in return is a hundred miles per hour. It seemed like they were in a rocket. The three of the kids had never been in a car going so fast, but Jeremy wasn't going faster than the rest of the cars; he was actually going much slower than the rest.

Sarah closed her eyes in the back seat, and Bobby could see her mumbling prayers. Bobby looked out the window and thought it was the coolest thing going that fast. Jason did too. The boys sat up high and took it all in. Jeremy laughed and said, "Hey, before I drop you off at the park, I need to swing by my boyfriends if you don't mind."

Jason nodded his head saying, "Sure, it's okay, go right ahead." Bobby looked at Jason as Jason looked in the back seat and frowned his eyebrows in confusion. Jeremy flew down the Fway then made a turnoff and came up to a digital stop sign then turned right then left and continued around and came up to a hotel or motel-looking building and stopped. He told the kids, "Hold tight, I'll be right back, my friend lives on the third floor."

<h1 style="text-align:center">CHAPTER 29</h1>

———

As he left closing his car door, he hopped out and ran up to a building that had a spiral staircase. The kids sat in the car and looked up the third floor and noticed Jeremy there talking to some people. They watched a lot of people hanging out talking and laughing. "It seems like their having a big party," Bobby said.

"Our parents would never allow us to attend a big party where we didn't know anyone," Sarah whispered.

About fifteen minutes later, Jeremy came back down and to the car with a friend. "Hey, guys, meet my friend." He opened the car door and introduced his friend, "Hey, meet my buddy, Chad!" Chad looked into the car at the kids and asked them, "Hey, kids, are you thirsty and hungry?"

Jeremy blurted out, "Chad is throwing a killer party!" Chad handed the kids a little baggie one at a time as they hopped out of the car. The kids were all confused as they looked at the small bags Chad gave them.

Sarah said, "It's water."

"Oh my gosh!" Bobby blurted out.

Jason replied, "Cool!"

As the kids followed Jeremy and Chad up to the building, they listened to them talking, and it seemed they were speaking a foreign language. Bobby whispered to Jason and Sarah, "What is killer party, cool, dude?"

Sarah said, "I know, they called me dude. They know I'm a girl, right!"

Jeremy shouted out, "Follow us to the third floor, guys!"

"Hey, guys!" Chad yelled out. "We q'd all kinds of meat, so dive in, kids!"

Jason anxiously whispered to Jeremy that they ran out of money. He replied, "Don't worry about that, kid." Jeremy grabbed plates and handed them to the kids. "You guys eat whatever you want, and the drinks are in that blue ice chest over by the fridge."

The kids' eyes opened wide as they saw the food table. It looked like a dinner table fit for a king. Bobby excitable mentioned to Jason and Sarah, "Oh my gosh, look at all the food." Bobby started naming off all the food, "Chicken, beef, ribs, hotdogs, potato salad, macaroni salad, regular salad, spaghetti, Chinese noodles and rice, cookies, cake, Jell-O—you name it, guys, they have it!"

The kids piled their plates so high with so much food. Jeremy came back around the corner and chuckled and said, "Hey, guys, get a couple of plates. However much you want, guys." Sarah's plate had mostly desserts.

"Did you guys get your soda baggie?" Jeremy asked.

Jason replied, "Oh yeah, we forgot."

Jeremy suggested, "The purple bag, it's grape, kids, yum!" Jeremy stepped through out of sight. Bobby grabbed three bags from the ice chest, and they all walked through the living room and sat on the floor. They all looked at their soda baggie and read out the flavors.

"Cool, eh, guys?" Jason asked.

"So weird," Sarah mumbled.

The music was blaring on songs they've never heard before. There were approximately twenty-five to thirty people inside Chad's place. They were dancing, eating, laughing, and drinking special drinks. The kids finished up with all their food thirty minutes later. Bobby yelled out, "I'm so stuffed, guys," and leaned back and fell over. Jason and Sarah laughed at Bobby and said, "We are too!" Shortly after that, a girl with blonde spikey hair came into the living room and sat next to the kids and blurted out, "Hey!" She introduced herself to the kids as Casper.

Bobby asked, "Like the ghost?" Jason shoved Bobby to shut up. Jason apologized.

Casper laughed and said, "Yes, Bobby, Casper the friendly ghost."

Bobby and Jason blurted out at the same time, "Cool!" Casper then asked if they were having a nice time. They all blurted out, "Yes, we are."

Sarah said, "We appreciate everything." Casper then asked each of their names and where they lived. They each named off their names, then Jason blurted out that they live in the country. Bobby then said, "Our parents dropped us off in the city to go check out a movie."

Casper excitably said, "What movie did you see?"

Bobby shouted, "*Wonder Woman's Revenge*! I love her!"

Casper laughed and agreed, "I love her too, and I can't wait to see that movie too!" She got up and told the kids, "Well, have a good time. If you get thirsty or hungry, go help yourselves." They all did a hand wave and said thank you. Jeremy and Chad came back there and told the kids that they could leave in fifteen minutes. Jeremy told the kids to meet him down by his car and that he would be down shortly. Five minutes later, the kids got up and started walking down to the car. While they all walked down to the car, Jeremy and Chad were discussing another party they were going to have next weekend.

Jeremy then opened up his fancy car with what he called a car alarm. It made a chirp beep. The kids then piled back into Jeremy's car, and they all said thank you to Chad for all the food and party. Chad replied, "You're welcome, kids, nice meeting you all."

Jeremy asked the kids where they wanted to be dropped off. Jason replied quickly, "At that park you picked us up at."

Jeremy then asked what the kids were going to do after he dropped them off. "Just hang out until our parents come for us," Sarah replied. They shortly arrived at the park. Jeremy came to the park and stopped, and the kids hopped out and shouted "Thank you." They started running to the center of the park. They didn't even look back. They were so eager to get back home.

CHAPTER 30

They finally got to where they had entered this year and sat down quickly. Bobby asked, "Hey do you have the card and dice?"

Jason replied, "Yes, I do." Jason asked, "Do you have the pocket watch, Bobby?"

"Yes, I do," Sarah blurted out. "I have my necklace, I've kept it in my pocket the whole time." They all were so excited to return home that they couldn't believe it's only been one day that they've been there. One day seemed like a lifetime there; shocked from seeing all the new technology and people. They had wished they could bring back something to share but didn't have any money to buy anything, so they sat around in a triangle and held hands. They had put their items at the center. Jason placed the ace card down and had the dice in his hands. As they held hands, they whispered, "It's time to go, time to go, why we are here, nobody knows, take us home for it's time to go." As they chanted over and over, they all were thinking of 1945. As they chanted over and over, "Time to go, time to go," the wind started picking up. As the wind started to swirl violently, Jason released one of his hands. Sarah grabbed his arm, and Jason threw the dice; it bounced and hit snake eyes. A one on each dice, and a puff of smoke and wind swirled around and *poof*! They disappeared from the park. They ended back at the baseball field in their home town in 1945. They opened their eyes holding hands and felt so relieved and scared and sad all at the same time. "We didn't find Jody, you guys," Sarah replied.

Bobby said with a sad face, "I know, I can't believe this. How can we get back there? What do the numbers mean on the dice? I wish we could figure out the correlation between the numbers."

"I know that we rolled doubles each time. I'm just scared to continue to keep doing it, ending up all over the place, and what if one time, it doesn't work, then what?" Jason answered.

CHAPTER 31

They all gathered their items, and they started walking back home. Sarah mumbled, "I wonder if the six is the number that if you add the last numbers then subtracted the first number, it makes the number roll.

"No, that doesn't make much sense, or does it?" Jason asked. Jason then said, "Maybe I can try to work on that tonight when I get home. I feel super tired though, guys. Do you guys as well?"

Bobby said, "Yes, I'm so exhausted. I want to go to sleep right now."

Sarah laughed and said, "I agree, I want to sleep a whole week from all this time traveling crap. I know tonight I'll sleep like a baby."

"Me too," Jason added! They got to the fork on the road of their street and parted their ways. As Bobby was walking down Wilks Street, he totally forgot where he was and which house he was about to pass when there came up two cats. He said, "Oh, hey, little kittens," then froze; he had just realized where he was. He stopped in his steps and took a big gulp of his saliva. His eyes all bugged out and frightened to even see anyone. He heard some wind chimes ringing. He tried to move, but from fear, it kept his feet planted. He noticed the three ladies sitting down at a round table up on the wooden porch. He looked slowly over at them and tried to be quiet and not disturb their focus.

So Bobby hit the ground and started crawling all along the side of the wooden fence. He got up to the fence gate and paused then looked through the cracks to see if they heard him. It appeared that they didn't hear or see him, so he scurried across the sidewalk then continued down the side of the fence coming to the end. He continued to crawl all along the bottom turning left at the corner. As he looked back, he stopped to rest, then all of a sudden, three wooden broom handles slammed right down in front of him. Bobby screamed then started to stand up to run but couldn't move. Then all of a sudden, the three ladies started to whirl their broomsticks around over the top of Bobby. Bobby closed his eye, fearing what was next. The wind started to stir around, the wind chimes under their porch started to ring. The women started whispering words that seemed like a different language, chanting over and over then laid the tip of the broomstick onto Bobby's back and shoulders, and a unknown force took over his body. Bobby stood up not on his own will, then the three women drew him closer then whispered into his face, "Where are our belongings? You have our belongings."

Bobby's face was full of fright and replied, "I don't have them, I don't!"

"Yessss, you do, Bobby!"

"What items are you talking about?" Bobby asked with tears whaling up in his eyes.

"The pocket watch, the necklace, the silver mirror, and the clock."

"What?" Bobby said. "Those items we found at the dump are not yours."

"Yes, they are! And we want them now!"

"Well, I don't have them, you better let me go, or I'm going to tell my mom and dad!" Bobby yelled.

They all said in an angry voice, "You better get all the items, or we will turn you into a cat. All of you that have our items, you better have them by Monday." Bobby started to struggle around to break away from the three women as he dropped to the ground. The women told him that he better drop the items off by Monday, or he and his friends would be banished into cats like the rest of the cats.

Bobby then turned and started running home. Tears flowed down his face as he ran straight home. Bobby finally got home and ran straight to his bedroom. He slammed his door shut and laid in bed face down. He started to cry, so he put his pillow over his head. His mom heard him come in and slam his door. She went to his door and knocked and asked if Bobby was okay.

"Yeah, Mom," Bobby yelled out. "I'm fine. Just lying down for a little bit, it's been a long day. I'll come out in a little bit."

"Okay, Bobby, if you're hungry for a snack, I made some cookies."

"Okay, Mom, thank you." Bobby laid there for a little bit, then fell asleep. He woke up after about thirty minutes in a panic, thinking he was still captured by the three women who looked like witches. He quickly pulled out the pocket watch from his pocket and threw it over on his desk and whispered to himself, "I never want to touch that watch Again! I have to go tell Jason and Sarah. How am I going to tell my mom, though?" He thought of a way to get out of the house. He grabbed the comic books and headed out the door and started to walk outside to get his bicycle.

Bobby's mother yelled out, "Where do you think you're going, Bobby!"

Bobby replied, "I'm just gonna take these comic books over to my friend Adam. I shouldn't be long, Mom, I promise."

"Okay, be sure to be back within forty-five minutes, supper is almost ready."

"Okay, Mom." Bobby shut the door and grabbed his bike and pedaled down his street and over to Jason's house. He knocked on the front door, and Jason's mom came to the door.

"Hi, Mrs. Ferrahi, can I speak to Jason for a quick second?"

"Sure," she replied, "come right in, he's in his room." Bobby walked down the hall and went right to Jason's room and knocked on the door.

Jason said, "Come in."

Bobby flew in and shut the door. Bobby then said, "Oh my god, Jason, when I was walking home, I didn't realize I was walking on *Wilks* street. Wilks street!" Jason yelled.

"What the heck are you doing on that street, Bobby!"

"I know, I know," Bobby replied. "I was so tired of the travel thing that I wasn't even paying attention until it was too late, but listen! The three ladies that we've seen were there, and they stopped me, and-and—" Bobby stuttered. "They put their brooms on me and told me to give back their items. I yelled, 'I don't have your items.' They all said, 'Yes you do. You and your three other friends.' I said, 'No.' They then named the items that we found at the junkyard. I then told them, 'We found those items at the junkyard.' They then demanded us to give them back by Monday or else they are going to turn us into cats."

"Oh my god, Jason, cats! That explains all the cats lingering around! Can you believe it?"

"*No!* Jason yelled.

"I can't believe it, what are we gonna do, Jason?" asked bobby. "We're giving the items back!"

What about Jody?" Jason then asked.

Bobby said with a question, "Jody? Oh my gosh, I totally forgot about Jody! I don't know, Jason. If we don't get the items to the witches, those three ladies, they're gonna turn us into cats, and I don't want to be a cat, do you?"

"*No!*" Jason answered.

Bobby said, "We're gonna have to gather the items and put them in a box and set them on their front porch. I don't want any problems. I'm tired of traveling back and forth through time. I don't want to do it anymore. I feel so bad about Jody, but we just can't risk trying to go back to the 1500s to save her."

"I agree," Jason answered. "Okay, I got to go now, my mom almost didn't let me leave the house. Should I tell Sarah now or wait for tomorrow on the bus?"

"Yeah, just wait until the bus, and we'll talk to her then."

"Okay, Bobby, thanks for coming over and for telling me. I will be thinking of everything that we've been going through. See you tomorrow on the bus."

"Okay, buddy, good night," Jason blurted out to Bobby as he walked out of his room to the front door.

"See ya, Jason." Bobby waved then got on his bike and rode all fast back home. When he was getting close to his driveway, he saw Adam outside throwing the ball. Bobby reached under his sweatshirt and pulled out Adam's comic books. "Here you go, Adam, I really enjoyed your comic books. I didn't finish reading them all, it's just that I've been so busy lately, and well, I didn't want you to worry about them, so here you are, I'll check out more of your comic books maybe this weekend if you don't have any plans."

"Okay, sure," Adam replied. "You okay, Bobby?"

"Yeah, I'm okay, I just have a lot on my mind, and weird stuff has happened, and I don't know how to talk about it, well, at least right now. Maybe someday, I'll tell you everything."

"Oh, okay."

"Well, I'll talk to you later, Adam, my mom is expecting me to be there right now for supper."

"Yeah, my mom too. My dad is supposed to be home tonight. I'm pretty excited since I haven't seen my dad in a month."

"Oh yeah, that's super neat, Adam. Well, I'll see you at school tomorrow."

"Okay, Bobby. Goodnight!" Adam finished then walked into his garage.

CHAPTER 32

Bobby rode back to his house, put his bike at the back then walked into the house from the backyard. He washed his hands in the restroom next to the service porch then walked into the kitchen and asked his mom if his dad was home.

She said, "Yes, he's in the room changing his clothes for dinner, go ahead, have a seat, he'll be right here."

Bobby tried to stay focused with his parents; he knew that if he acted any way out of sorts, they'd ask a lot of questions, and that is something Bobby didn't want to do, especially tonight after everything that has happened. Bobby's dad came to the table, and his mom sat the dishes of food in the middle and then sat down.

"Mmmmm, my favorite," Bobby said. "Chicken! I love your fried chicken and mashed potatoes, Mom! I can probably eat six pieces." Bobby's mom picked two pieces and sat them on Bobby's plate. "Mmm, a drumstick." Bobby grabbed the chicken drumstick and started eating it all fast. "Next," he blurted out.

Bobby's mom and dad looked at him strangely and said, "Slow down, mister, you're gonna choke."

"Oh yeah, okay, Dad, Mom! I'm just super hungry. We did a lot of running at school and after school today."

"Oh yeah?" Bobby's dad asked, "So how was your day, Bobby?"

"Oh. it was pretty good, nothing too exciting happened today. Tomorrow, I think Ms. White is supposed to show a film during the half of the class, then we have to write about it over the weekend."

"Oh, that sounds interesting.

"Yeah, sounds fun to me." Bobby's parents kind of laughed and then carried on a little conversation between the two of them about each of their days. What Bobby wanted to do was eat then go right to bed, so he ate some potatoes then asked for some green beans. His mother scooped out a nice helping then continued to talk with Bobby's dad.

"Uh, excuse me, Mom and Dad, can I ask you a question?"

"Sure, Bobby," his dad answered.

"Uh, do you remember the house on Wilks and Fifth avenue?"

"Uh, the one that's all boarded up?"

"Uh, yeah, uh, that's the one. Well, does anybody live there?"

His mom asked him, "Didn't you ask me about that a few weeks ago?"

"Yes, Mom. It's just that I saw all these cats hanging around, and if they're hanging around, wouldn't someone be living there to take care of them?"

"I don't think so, Bobby. I walk around the block when you're at school for exercise before work, and I never have seen any cats or people there."

"Oh! I was just wondering, Dad, if you knew who lived there."

"Uh, I thought about twenty-plus years ago that a couple or someone lived there but then was found dead in the house, that's why it wasn't sold and is abandoned."

"Oh, okay, Dad, are you sure?"

"No, Bobby, I'm not sure, but I'm sure the hall of records would know about that house."

Bobby asked, "Do you think three ladies, possibly sisters, live there or lived there."

"Perhaps, but I kind of doubt it."

Bobby could tell they didn't want to talk about that at all, so he just smiled and continued eating after he said thanks and that he was just wondering about the house. After three pieces of fried chicken and potatoes and green beans, Bobby said he was all done and asked to be excused. "I have to take a bath before bed, mom, do you mind?"

She replied, "No, it's okay, son."

"Love you, Mom and Dad, thank you for dinner, it was delicious!" Then Bobby went to the restroom to take a bath. He drew the water to a warm temperature then slipped in and soaked for a good twenty minutes. He washed up then pulled the plug on the drain. He laid there as the water drained. He continued to lay there and thought of Hollywood and then Jody. He couldn't help but feel heartbroken for Jody. He was never gonna see Jody again who was banished off the earth, and there was nothing he could do. It was impossible since the witches wanted all of the items. So Bobby made a prayer for Jody and hoped that she was happy in her new life, and if there was any way to return to her and bring her home, he would. He kissed his hand and put it to his chest and closed his eyes and whispered, "This is for you, my love, Jody'. I'll never forget you." Tears fell from his eyes as he laid there then realized that the water was almostly completely drained. He then wrapped the towel around his waist then picked up his dirty clothes and opened the bathroom door and walked over to his room and shut his door. Bobby got into his pajamas then slipped under the covers into bed. He reached over and shut the little lamp on his nightstand off then turned to his side and closed his eyes. Bobby fell right to sleep. He was so exhausted from everything that happened. All three kids fell right to sleep.

CHAPTER 33

The next morning came. They all woke to their alarm clocks buzzing. They got ready and had their breakfast then grabbed their jackets then walked over to their bus stop and waited for the bus to pick them up. Shortly, the bus came along and picked up Sarah first, Jason, then Bobby. They all noticed that the new girl was being picked up again. They watched her get on the bus, and she walked right back to where their friend Jody sat. They stared at her with anger like she had no business sitting there. They didn't say anything to her; they just stared at her. Bobby's stop was next. They saw Bobby standing at his stop when the bus pulled up. The bus driver opened the door for him, and Bobby hopped on and walked to the back where Jason and Sarah were. Jason asked, "Hey, is the new kid Adam coming on the bus?"

Bobby looked out the windows and said, "Um, I forgot to ask him last night. I'll ask him today when we see him." Then about that time, he took a double take on the new girl sitting on Jody's seat. Bobby whispered to Jason, "Hey, what's this girl doing sitting on Jody's seat."

"I don't know. Should we say something?"

"No, Bobby, we should just let her sit there, it's a free world anyway, Jody isn't coming back."

So Bobby then changed the subject and asked Sarah, "Hey, Sarah, I had a run-in yesterday when I was walking home. I accidentally walked down Wilks Avenue, and the three witches stopped me and demanded the items that we found at the junkyard.

"What!" Sarah replied quietly. "Are you serious?"

"Yes, Sarah, I'm very serious! They told me if we don't bring those items to them, they are going to change all four of us into cats like the rest were. That explains all the cats. And you know what, I have never been more scared. They twirled their broom handles over me, and they restrained me without even touching me." The new girl turned her head to listen to what they were talking about.

She then said to Bobby when she turned around, "So you think witches live on Wilks and Fifth?"

"Uh, yeah. Those people aren't normal, and they look like witches."

She laughed and said, "Perhaps they are witches. They do exist!"

She then turned around, and behind her back, Bobby pointed at her and lipped to Jason and Sarah, "Who is she? What the heck is she saying?"

Sarah turned her head back and forth and lipped back to Bobby, "I don't *know*!"

Jason shrugged his shoulders and said, "Oh, we're pulling into the school parking lot, we'll talk at lunch, okay!" So the bus stopped and parked. The bus driver opened the doors, and the kids started piling off the bus and walked to their classes. The new girl gathered her items then stood up then started to walk off the bus. Bobby went behind her and then Sarah, then Jason was the very last person following Sarah. The new girl then stopped and turned and said, "So you're Bobby?"

Bobby looked puzzled. "Uh, yea. Who are you?" he asked. She ignored him, turned back around, and then walked off the bus to her class. They all stayed back, walking slowly to Ms. White's class. Bobby then said to Jason and Sarah, "What a snot she is. Who does she think she is, you guys?"

"I know, why would she ask if you were Bobby then not answer your question as to who she is!"

"I don't know, I just don't think I like her very much," Sarah added. Shortly, they noticed that that girl walked into Ms. White's class and sat down at Jody's seat. The three of them walked in after her and then stopped when they saw the girl sitting at Jody's seat. It instantly made them mad, so they waited for Ms. White to tell her that the new girl was sitting at the wrong desk. Ms. White looked at the seating chart and said, "Noooo, she's at the right desk and chair, now go sit down, kids." Ms. White tapped on the chalkboard with her big flower ring on her right hand to get everybody's attention and spoke loudly, "I have a lot to cover about halfway through class. I want to show you all a film, and I'll explain. Just go sit down at your seats, kids." As they sat down, they glared at the girl.

She looked up but didn't have any expression on her face at all. Ms. White tapped the front chalkboard again and said, "Excuse me, class, I need you to take home these papers. Can I have your help, Sarah?"

Sarah replied, "Sure, Ms. White!" Sarah got up and walked over to Ms. White and started handing out the papers that Ms. White handed her. Then Ms. White said softly, "I need you guys to take these medical cards home and have your parents fill them out and sign and bring them back. Next week, we will be giving smallpox shots to everybody, starting with the As then going through the alphabet to the Zs, so, Sarah, can you also hand these out?"

"Sure, Ms. White."

"Now, I'd like to start a film, it's about twenty-five minutes long, then I want you to go home and over the weekend, write me two pages about the film and return them on Monday. Okay?"

The class all replied, "Okay."

"So now, I will start the roll call, then we will open our books to page 180 and read five pages." Ms. White started the roll call; everybody answered, and Ms. White would look up to make sure she saw the right kid with the right name. She then called Jody Jenkins. Sarah stopped in her tracks and felt a stabbing sickening pain in her stomach. Bobby and Jason both looked up with fear in their eyes. Nobody answered the first time, then Ms. White called again, and the new girl raised her hand and said, "I'm sorry, Ms. White. Yes, I'm here."

Bobby fell out of his seat and yelled, "What the heck are you saying! You're not Jody Jenkins!"

"*Yes, I am, Bobby!*"

"Nooooooo, you're not, quit acting like you're *Jody*!"

Ms. White walked over quickly and said, "What's wrong with you, Bobby, stop shouting at Jody."

"No, Ms. White, this isn't Jody Jenkins."

"Yesssssss, Bobby, it is!" His jaw dropped as Jason's and Sarah's.

"What?" Jason asked. "Jody Jenkins? You live with your grandma?"

"Yes, I live with my grandma, who do you live with, Jason?"

"You know my name?" he asked her again.

"Yes, I know your name, we've been in the same class all year!"

Ms. White bent down and said to Bobby and Jason, "I don't know what's wrong with you, fellas, today, but you better straighten up before I send you to the principal's office."

They both sat up and said, "Yes, Ms. White," then sat back on their chairs and just stared at Jody.

They wanted to ask, Is that you in there? Where's the other Jody? How come you look so different? Questions like that. Sarah walked back to her seat next to Jody like she had just seen a ghost. She slowly looked over at Jody and slightly smiled and then asked Jody, "Do we hang out together?"

Jody said, "Uh, we have a few times."

What the heck is going on? Sarah thought to herself. "I can't believe any of this. I sure don't feel too good," Sarah softly said to herself. The class continued, and Bobby couldn't stop staring at Jody.

This new Jody was a pretty girl, but it was someone who they did not know; someone that they had never seen in their lives. So they sat and waited for eight thirty to come. They couldn't read the five pages;

all they could do was stare at "new" Jody and think about everything that they had been through.

"This totally changes up everything," Jason whispered to Bobby.

"I know, I know," Bobby answered. The film started, and Bobby, Jason, and Sarah sat and stared at the new Jody the whole time.

Jason leaned over to Jody and said, "Are you going to meet us today at the cafeteria like we all do and all meet every single day?"

Jody looked at Jason and said, "Not today, I have a doctor's appointment."

"Oh," Jason said with a weird look on his face. Jason then took his hands and grabbed his face and pulled it down to the top of the desk and just sat there staring at the darkness down in his hands. Bobby and Jason just kept running their hands back and forth on their faces backtracking the events that had taken place with the other Jody and the gang.

How could this be right? How can we carry on forward when life isn't the same without our friend Jody, the one Jody that we're used to." You could see Sarah crying in the dark as the film played. Soon, the film was completed. Ms. White walked over to the movie camera and flipped the reels and clicked the switch to rewind the film. The film rewound quickly, and when it reached the end, the film flapped making a slapping sound. The three of them—Jason, Bobby, and Sarah—stared into their desks in dismay, slowly realizing that life was going to be different this day forward and that they'd never forget their best friend Jody.

After the film, Ms. White turned on the lights and then mentioned again to have the medical cards filled out and be brought back then dismissed the whole class. Jason, Bobby, and Sarah mumbled softly to each other, "Let's meet at Jason's house after school and get all the items together so that we can give them to the witches on Wilks Street, okay! It's obvious that Jody is never coming back."

The three of them gave a slight hug and hung their heads in sadness as they walked to their next class. The rest of the day was a cloudy haze. Nothing made sense, everything sounded like it was muffled as if the world was closing down around them, suffocating their thoughts of reality. At lunch, they hardly ate a bite and just stared off to the distance, picking at their food like little birds. Every time one of them started to say something out loud, they'd say, "Oh, never mind, I forgot what I was going to say." The bell rang, and they all stood up like zombies, dumped their trash, and started walking to their last classes. They got to the hall and split with a soft numb reply, "See you guys at the bus after school." They waved and marched to their classes. After a few hours, two forty-five came, and the bell rang to dismiss everybody from school. The gang met up at the bus and sat on their usual spot in silence as the driver shut the doors when all the kids got in and sat down. The bus driver pulled away from the school's circled driveway and started driving and stopping at everybody's stop. They first went through town. Jason would always see who was at his pa's deli. Once in a great while, he'd see his uncle or his pa and wave, hoping to get noticed, but today, he didn't even look up.

CHAPTER 34

The bus stopped at Bobby's stop then Jason's and Sarah's. They all walked home the rest of the way and grabbed their items from their rooms to go to Jason's house to put into the *golden box*. Bobby grabbed the pocket watch, and Sarah grabbed the beautiful necklace and walked over to Jason's house and waited outside. Jason grabbed the clock and the box. Jason opened the front door and said, "You guys can come in, and we'll go through to the garage." They both got up from sitting and went with Jason. Jason already had the box on one of his dad's workbenches, and Bobby and Sarah set their stuff inside. Jason had taken out all the other miscellaneous stuff and only had the items that had the initials engraved on them. Sarah spoke softly, "Wonder what these initials mean?"

Bobby said nervously, "I'm not sure if we wanna know any more about these items or people."

Jason said, "Okay, now that we have the stuff altogether, what are we gonna do about the mirror that Jody had?"

Sarah said, "Remember I grabbed it? It's right here. I grabbed it when I saw that she left it behind from the time traveling to in 1515.

"Cool," Bobby blurted out!

"Let's go, I'm so scared, you guys, you just don't know," Bobby spoke nervously. The three of them got the box and started to walk down and over to Wilks Street. They were silent the whole walk up until they could see the house in the near distance.

"Okay," Jason said, "so let's just open the gate and take the box up to the front door, ring the doorbell, and then run off, sound good?"

Bobby and Sarah replied, "Yes!"

So they got within thirty feet of the house, and Bobby said with fright in his voice and eyes, "I don't want to do this, I don't want to do this, I don't want to do this!"

Jason, with a stern voice, said, "Snap out of it, Bobby, we have to do this."

Sarah grabbed Jason's arm as they got to the creaky wooden gate, and Bobby grabbed Sarah's arm. Their steps were in synch, trying not to make a sound as they opened the gate, then started up the path that had dirt and leaves all over as the grass was overgrown, unmanicured, and dead looking. Jason mumbled softly, "Now let's walk this up here, and then as soon as we set it down and ring the doorbell, we run, ready!"

"Yes," Sarah and Bobby whispered. They took one step up the wooden step then the second step as to pause with each step taken. Jason whispered, "Four more steps, guys!" They called off each step up until the last floor, and they froze with fear. "Okay," Jason said, "let's just slowly walk up, set this down, and ring the doorbell." As they stepped up to the door, the box of items started to chatter as if Jason was shaking from fear. They stepped closer to the door, and a board creaked. They stopped in their tracks, looked around fearfully, then continued forward. Just as they got close up to the door, the box of items started to shake; Jason's face went from light brown to white. Bobby and Sarah blurted out, "What's wrong, Jason?"

He replied, "I don't know, I'm not shaking this box, and I can't move!"

Bobby said, "Oh my gosh, it's happening again!"

Sarah blurted out, "What, what's going on?" About that time, the wind chimes hanging started to chime, the wind picked up as if it was whistling. Cats started to appear out of thin air. The kids held each other tightly with their eyes all bugged out. Sarah started to cry and mumbled, "I wanna go home." Tears whaled up in Bobby and Jason's eyes. Then they heard footsteps. *Click, clack, click, clack, thump. Click, clack, click, clack, thump.* It almost sounded like horses galloping. Then out of nowhere, two women appeared at the end of the wooden porch. The box was suspended in the air as the three looked with fright at the ladies. They were mumbling a chant as they walked closer.

Bobby yelled out and pleaded, "I brought the items that you asked for! We don't have anything else. Please let us go, we didn't do anything wrong, we were just collecting items, we had no idea of anything." Then down at the gate, another lady appeared. She stood ground as to protect the gate from anybody running out. Sarah buried her head into Jason's arm as the two ladies got close and opened the box. The two of them whispered as to smile and chant words of a different language. The other lady next to the gate started walking up the steps to join her sisters in a ritual chant. The kids dropped to the floor, and when they did, they started to crawl toward the steps. The three women were so enthralled with the items of the box that they didn't even notice that the kids were escaping and crawling away down the steps.

As they got to the path that headed to the gate, Jason stepped on a broken branch that snapped loudly. They all turned around with a glare. Their eyes looked like they were headlights piercing yellowish red in color. The three kids froze in their spot. Bobby yelled out, "Leave us alone, we brought your stuff back, so leave us alone!"

Sarah pulled Jason's and Bobby's arms and made it through the gate as it slammed behind them. They fell just past the gate on the sidewalk, then got up and started to run back toward Jason's house.

The wind was so fierce that they could hardly see the houses. They were caught in a whirlwind but held on tight to each other as they made it across the street. They looked back and noticed a swirled purple and white light hanging over the top of the house. As the three kids ran farther and farther away from the house, they felt the weight off their shoulders. As they got back to Jason's house, they flew into his house, running as to never wanting to stop.

They ran right into Jason's mom. She said sternly, "Hey, slow down, what's the hurry?"

They all stopped cold and out of breath, and Jason replied, "Oh, sorry, Mom, we were just outside running around."

She replied, "It's okay, is everything okay?"

"Yes, Mama, we're okay." She stared them all down as they stared up at her.

As they did, Jason's mom said, "Oh my goodness, you guys have a bloody nose, come here into the bathroom now!" The three of them took their hands to their nose and wiped across to see the blood. "Now, Jason Ferrahi, you tell me right now what is going on!"

Jason pleaded, "Nothing, Mama, nothing! We were just running around, the wind got so high and dusty, that's all, Mama, seriously!"

"Well, I think it's time for Bobby and Sarah to head home, perhaps I'll take you in the car so I can speak to your parents." As the three of them held tissues under their noses, Jason's mom said, "Jason, you stay here and take a bath."

Jason blurted out, "Oh no, I don't wanna stay here by myself, Mama, I wanna go, please let me go!"

Jason's mom's eyes had a worried look in them and replied, "Oh, okay, Jason, let's go!" They all walked in a straight line after Mrs. Ferrahi and got in the car that was parked in the garage. Jason pulled up the garage door as his mom backed the car up. Jason fastened the garage and ran to the side of the car and got in and sat in the back seat with Sarah and Bobby.

Jason whispered to the two of them, "Don't mention anything, okay? We'll just forget this all happened, okay?" They all grabbed each other's hands and looked into each other's eyes to agree with a nod that this would be the last day that they would ever see or mention the *golden box* again.

The *end*.

Written by Cassie A. Hunter-Macedo

The *end*.

About the Author

Cassie is a fifty-year-old writer of German Irish descent. She was born on December 31, 1969, in Fresno, California. She has survived with the help of her mom, Coleena Macedo, and her one and only older sister by two years, Felicia Strole. The support of her mom, sister, family, and wife, Sarah Fuentes, has gotten her this far. She has a degree in associates science in radiology technology and worked in a trauma level III hospital, taking X-rays until a hand injury. She had several unfortunate injuries since the hand injury on the job and several surgeries that changed her career dramatically. She had survived many debilitating health issues like learning how to rewalk, relearn how to eat, and talk again through the support of these three powerful women and her family. She is an artist who uses pen, pencil, and acrylic paint and has done several large murals locally at the Fresno County Court House and several different people's and children's rooms at their residences. She's also done all the murals at the Kidz Can 2 Center, all after she graduated high school and college. She enjoys fast cars, old classic cars, scary movies, and old classic cartoons. She especially enjoys spending time with her wife and family and her seven furry babies—three dogs and four cats. She loves all primates, and she is a true animal lover. She loves to cook. She enjoys cooking Italian, Mexican, Chinese food, and BBQ. Some good ol' tri-tip steak and a rack of ribs. Her heroes would be first, her mom, who is incredible in all aspects and is extremely strong-willed and young at heart, then her sister, who has guided her all through her life, enforcing positive mental being. Third would be her beautiful, strong, funny, and young-at-heart wife. These three have molded her into who she is today. Her other heroes are as follows: Albert Einstein, Michael Angelo, Amelia Earhart and, last but not the least, Jane Goodall.